In the foyer before you is an iron door, set firmly into the wall. To the side is a set of stone stairs, spiraling down into the earth, perhaps to the dungeon, you think. Lord Fear has probably hidden the crystal skull deep under the castle, where he feels the most comfortable.

But the iron door looks like the entrance to the castle treasury, and the chances are equally as good that the skull has been placed inside.

The choice is yours.

If you open the vault, go to 4.

If you go down the stone stairs, go to 60.

You make the decisions on your way to adventure within the *Dungeon of Fear*!

RUGBY LIBRARY,

ST. MATTHEWS STREET,

RUGBY. CV21 3BZ

Tel. RUGBY 571813

011606942 3

Endless Quest® BOOKS

Dungeon of Fear
Michael Andrews

Castle of the Undead
Nick Baron

Secret of the Djinn
Jean Rabe
May

Siege of the Tower
Kem Antilles
July

A Wild Ride
Louis Anderson
September

Forest of Darkness
Michael Andrews
November

Endless Quest BOOKS

DUNGEON OF FEAR

Michael Andrews

Always
__for Maria,__
my ghostess with the mostest,
who turns every day into Halloween,
and who loves her pirates as much as I love my
mansion

and

__for Jim and Ken,__
friends and brothers.

DUNGEON OF FEAR

Copyright ©1994 TSR, Inc.
All Rights Reserved.

All characters in this book are fictitious. Any resemblance to actual persons, living or dead, is purely coincidental.

This book is protected under the copyright laws of the United States of America. Any reproduction or other unauthorized use of the material or artwork herein is prohibited without the express written permission of TSR, Inc.

Random House and its affiliate companies have worldwide distribution rights in the book trade for English language products of TSR, Inc.

Distributed to the book and hobby trade in the United Kingdom by TSR Ltd.

Distributed to the toy and hobby trade by regional distributors.

Cover art by Jeff Easley.

Interior art by Terry Dykstra.

ENDLESS QUEST is a registered trademark owned by TSR, Inc. DRAGON STRIKE and the TSR logo are trademarks owned by TSR, Inc.

All TSR characters, character names, and the distinctive likenesses thereof are trademarks owned by TSR, Inc.

First Printing: March 1994
Printed in the United States of America
Library of Congress Catalog Card Number: 93-61437

9 8 7 6 5 4 3 2 1

ISBN: 1-56076-835-5

TSR, Inc.
P.O. Box 756
Lake Geneva, WI 53147
United States of America

TSR Ltd.
120 Church End, Cherry Hinton
Cambridge CB1 3LB
United Kingdom

In this book, you are Kir Trelander, known among the populace of the realm as Shadow. You are barely a man, just come of age less than half a year ago, and you're still a little awkward around attractive women. You attended all the necessary schools, but at some point early in your young life, you realized that you wanted more than to be a simple merchant or warrior or scribe. You wanted—no, you craved—more than a normal life could give you. You needed romance. You needed intrigue.

You needed adventure.

In your mind, you could envision glories and wealth that no one else could imagine. In your mind, you understood that no two people were the same, that everyone was different—and that you were different from most.

And so, breaking all the strict rules that civilization had set for you, you became that which everyone despised, that which could let you roam free: a thief.

In your society, a thief is not always considered to be all that bad. And unlike a lot of thieves, you steal for a much more important reason than simply desiring an object: you steal only to provide those who have nothing with the simple comforts everyone deserves: life, a warm place to dwell, and food on the table. As much as you hate to admit it, you cannot allow yourself to make a profit off the things you steal. They must always go to benefit the greater good. Only a few months ago, with the help of a female thief, you saved an entire village from starvation. Perhaps your desire to do good is the reason you have never resolved the matter of the emerald collar—you simply don't know what to do with it.

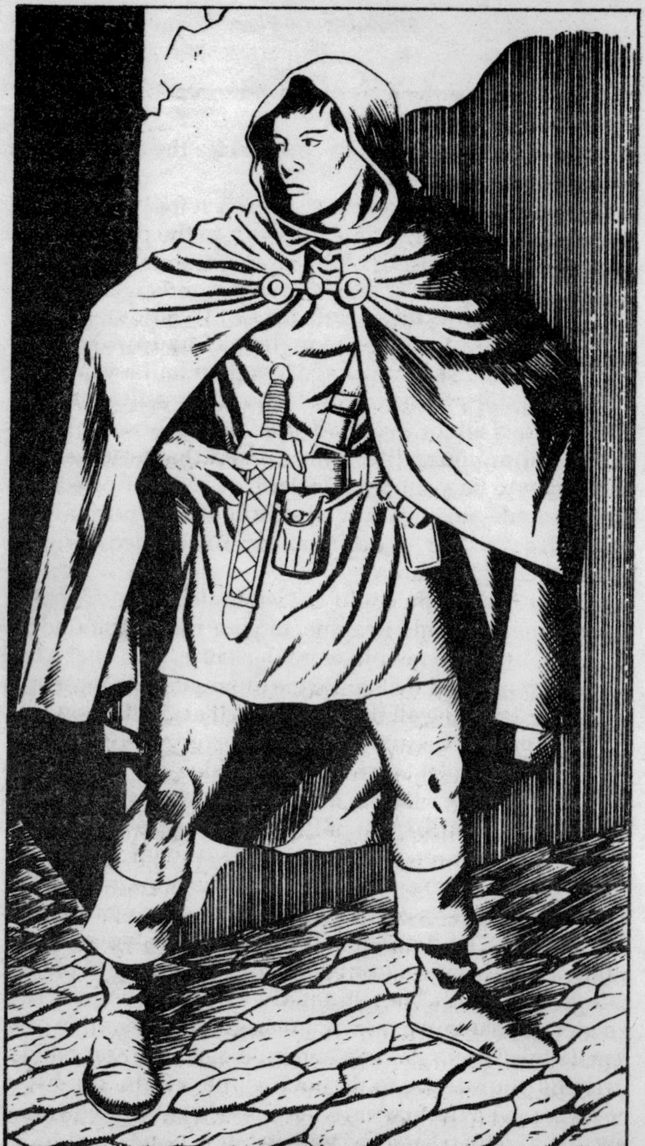

And, except for reasons of self-preservation, you never kill.

But you will be forced to re-evaluate these matters in just a very short time. . . .

You have been in your hut in the forest for too long. You decide that it is finally time to return to the people of the realm—the heat must be off by now. You stole the emerald collar at the royal ball, more than a month ago, and the royal guards—the king's elite squad known as the Red Dragons—cannot possibly be looking for you still, now can they?

Remember: This is not just a character you're reading about. Kir Trelander is you, and you have to make his choices as though his life—or your life—depends on it.

Good luck, Shadow. . . .

Go to 5.

1

You cannot pass up the opportunity to steal something right out of the king's vault. That wand looks valuable to you, as it appears to be made of precious crystal—it may even hold magical properties. The wand is only about six inches long, and the tip looks like pure silver, forged in the shape of a lithe woman or girl, whose four delicate wings spread out behind her as though she is in flight. You look closer. The wings are made with countless tiny holes in them, probably for decoration. You smile to yourself. The wand will bring you a lot of money on the black market—money that can be used to feed a lot of people in the poorer sections of the realm.

As the others file out the treasury door, you move quickly and palm the silver tip in your hand like a magician, hiding the length of the wand behind your wrist. You pretend to scratch your neck, and you drop the crystal rod down into your tunic, which is bulky enough to conceal such a small item.

You look up and pass through the doorway. No one noticed a thing.

Then you are in the anteroom, and the cleric moves past you to close the treasury door. Suddenly, he stops. "I sense . . . magic . . . about you," he says. "Why did I not sense this before?"

You shrug innocently and move deliberately to the far side of the room, trying to get close to the door to make a hasty escape. The cleric looks at you strangely, then points to your tunic. "He has stolen something! Arrest him!"

Dare is slow to respond, but after a second he lurches toward you. The treasury guards are halfway across the room when you pull the wand from your tunic. You hold the wand tightly in your hand and raise it high. "Stop!" you shout, "or I'll use it!"

The guards and the warrior stop where they are. Of course, you have no idea what the wand is or how to use it, but they don't know that—you hope.

The cleric approaches. "That is one of the keys to Faerie," he says. "It has never been used, for we do not know what kingdom will be open to us—one of the good kingdoms, or one of the evil. Please, just put the wand down, and I'll put it away, and you can get on with your quest. We can . . . overlook this problem. Please."

You look at the wand out of the corner of your eye—the thing sure is pretty, you think—and the light playing off the figurine's silver wings glimmers seductively.

Without knowing why, your head feels suddenly light, and something compels you to wave the wand above your head in a wide circle. Air rushes through the holes in the figure's silver wings, and the room reverberates with a high whistle.

Above you, a circle of radiant, bubbling energy appears, casting golden light upon you. You step away, and out of the soft light come hundreds upon hundreds of tiny, flitting shapes, all singing their peculiar, high-pitched song, their wings fluttering rapidly in the air.

The cleric and your companions stand amazed as the room fills with the inhabitants of Faerie: soft, radiant men and women whose song fills your heart with a numbing peace. A tiny woman flies to the palm of your outstretched hand and gazes up at you. Her hair is long and silken, cascading over her wispy body in rippling waves. Her body glows warmly with every beat of her heart, and she smiles at you, pulling her hair back to expose her long, pointed ears.

She opens her mouth and sings. Every muscle in your body relaxes, and you smile as her song seems to echo throughout your body.

Absently, you open your eyes and look toward your friends. They seem to be covered with fireflies. You want to shake your head to clear it, but you have not the strength to move. A dim part of your mind, befuddled by the hypnotic song of Faerie, understands that the thief and the warrior have been swarmed over by the sprites and denizens of Faerie. The cleric and the treasury warriors lay sprawled upon the floor, smiling blissfully, as the fairies congregate upon them.

Then you look down at yourself. They cover you completely, their thin bodies glowing with a sickly green hue, their wings buzzing furiously, like angry insects. The sprite from your hand suddenly flies in front of your face and hovers there, grinning at you. Her song grows in intensity, until it resembles a high-pitched growl that reverberates through your very bones. Then she opens her smiling mouth, and you notice for the first time how long and sharp her teeth are, and how her eyes glow an unearthly yellow.

You are cold and numb now, and you feel as though you are floating on a sea of soft clouds. You are barely aware of the fairy landing on your face and biting into your skin. Then the others swarming over you happily join the feast of your flesh, and in the seconds before you die and your soul is claimed by the shadow-dwellers of Faerie, you realize you should have heeded the cleric's warning.

For the wand was a key to Faerie, all right, but it opened onto one of the dark places, where even sunlight is afraid to go.

The last thing you see is the tiny female flitting merrily before your eyes.

She blows you a kiss, and the darkness of the grave envelops you.

The End

2

You look toward the moonlit silhouette of Castle Arnstadt and think for a moment, then turn back to gaze at the crypt of the Arnstadt family.

"It makes sense to me that Lord Fear would try to take the castle here, seeing as how he thinks he's the new Prince of Darkness," you say. "So whatever is inside the crypt, I don't think it means us any harm. If it had, we would have been attacked while we were in the Red Room."

The others cannot argue with your logic, and it is very obvious that curiosity will not permit any of you to leave without getting a look inside the crypt. The three of you hold your swords ready and enter the cemetery.

You plod across the graveyard, being careful not to trip or step into any of the now-unoccupied graves, and a light blanket of fog swirls in eddies around your feet, caressing the tombstones with ethereal tendrils of mist. The Arnstadt crypt looms ahead, and from within its depths you glimpse a hint of the witchlight's blue glow.

You reach out for the black iron gates and shake them. "Locked," you say. You look to Dare for help, then the lock makes a clacking sound deep inside and the iron-barred gates swing open of their own accord.

"I think we've been invited inside," you say, quietly. "Shall we go in?"

Dare grunts his approval, and Keela defiantly throws

back her long hair, as if to challenge her own fear. "Let's go," she says, tightening her grip on her sword.

Above ground, the crypt is nothing more than an entrance chamber where flowers can be placed and mourners can visit. But inside, a long staircase leads down into the earth, where the bodies of the Arnstadt family are interred. You dimly see the blue glow at the bottom of the stone steps, and you reach out with your hands to steady yourself as you make your way down the stairs.

Then a torch suddenly flares behind you—the thief remembered to bring her pack—and your party proceeds down the dusty, old steps in the warm glow of torchlight.

A single iron gate bars the entrance to the vault, and as you approach it unlatches, as though by an unseen hand, and swings open.

The thief's torch casts an orange glow throughout the square room, with engraved marble plaques covering the burial places for twenty seven coffins. All are markers for long-dead members of the Arnstadt family, some having lived and died over five centuries ago.

But the floating blue witchlight is gone.

"Where did it go?" Keela asks. "It could not have gotten past us."

"No, it didn't," you say. "And I don't think it is gone either. You point up, to a carving above the iron gate. You take the torch from Keela and raise it high, dispelling the shadows around the angled ceiling.

Above the door, carved in marble, you find the image of a bird, an iron ring held in its mouth. You gasp and spin around. Exactly opposite the bird, above a wall of markers, is a carving of a lion, holding a black iron ring between its fangs.

The dream of the gray bird and lion comes back to you, and you tell your friends exactly what you dreamt. "It means something," you tell them. "It was a clue, I believe, sent by whatever brought us here."

Dare steps over to the marble bird and reaches for the ring. "Maybe we should pull on it. Maybe something will happen."

His hand closes around the ring, and you shout "No! Perhaps it is the lion's ring we should pull. We don't know what my dream meant."

"Hold on!" Keela yells. "I'm not exactly sure you should be pulling on either of the rings. Maybe it might be best if we just leave right now, go back to the inn, get some rest, and keep on in the morning. For all we know, this may be just a wild ghost chase."

You have only two things to go on: the meaning of your dream and common sense, and both are at war with each other. You can't do anything until you're sure what is best.

But, unless you do something, you may never know.

If you pull the bird's ring, go to 71.

If you pull the lion's ring, go to 11.

If you return to the Red Room Inn, go to 46.

3

You look longingly at the sarcophagi and the coffin bound with chains. Your curiosity is great—after all, you are a thief, and the idea of hidden, sparkling gems intrigues you to no end. But the warnings of the spirits were clear, and you have no desire to challenge the dead any more tonight.

You leave the hidden room, its contents intact, and close the secret door by pulling again on the iron ring. It snaps off in your hand, and the secret room is forever beyond your grasp.

The march through the village is uneventful, and you return to the Red Room Inn knowing that the end of your quest is near. Succeed or fail, the castle is your goal in the morning, and you must decipher the ghosts' clues if you are somehow challenged by Lord Fear.

While Keela puts more logs on the fire to keep the inn warm, you look out the window and stare at the trees standing strangely in the road. Tomorrow, you think. We will have the skull tomorrow.

Then Keela takes the watch, and you snuggle in your bedroll and fall blissfully to sleep.

Go to 12.

4

You step to the iron door and try the latch. It is locked. You pull your dagger from your belt and insert it carefully into the lock. So far, the door seems unprotected by spells or traps, but you're being very careful not to find that out first-hand.

You feel the point of your narrow dagger push against the lock's tumblers. It takes you half a minute, but you push and twist the knife so that the lock springs open with a loud snap, and you smile proudly, shoving open the door.

Keela holds up a torch, and on the far wall inside the treasury, piles of gold glint brilliantly.

"This is it!" you say. "Gold and jewels! The skull must be in here!"

The three of you step inside the vault and approach the piles of gold. Behind you, the door swings shut on hidden springs, and the lock catches silently. You do not notice that there is no doorknob on this side.

You reach for a handful of gold, then jerk back your hand, scowling in distaste. The gold—and now your hand—is covered with a thick layer of sticky spiderwebs. Come to think of it, now that you look around, the whole room is draped with webs: long, billowy webs, far larger and stronger than webs any normal spider would make.

"Uh-oh," you say, holding your torch up. You look toward the ceiling.

It is black with spiders, rippling, alive. A score of the creatures, unnaturally huge, looks down at you with bulbous ebony eyes. At the approach of your torch, a spider leaps to the floor and scurries toward you. Its face is a grotesque assemblage of features. Sharpened teeth gleam wickedly inside its parody of a mouth, which is flecked with whitish venom.

As though on some unspoken signal, the other spiders hurl themselves from the webbed ceiling and fall upon you in a rain of chittering horror. Keela, covered with them, cries out. She screams in pain as they bite through her clothes and across her bare legs. Dare chops a huge spider in half with his broadsword, then he falls to his knees as three large arachnids bite into the back of his legs.

Then you scream out loud as a smaller spider, about the size of your hand, latches onto your forearm and sinks its fangs into your flesh.

You fall to your knees, the wound burning coldly. The spiders continue biting mercilessly, then they crawl away in a wave and return to their lair on the ceiling.

Your body tingles in cold, electric pain. You struggle to get up, but your joints feel stiff and achy, and you find that you cannot move.

You struggle to cry out, but you cannot even open your mouth. Too late, you realize that the spiders' bites were full of a horrifying venom, and now you are paralyzed—perhaps for the rest of your life.

* * * * *

You try to move for hours, but only a few of your five senses are active. You sleep for a while, then wake to discover that the spiders have started spinning webs around you and your companions, preparing to turn you into a living source of food for them, these spiders from the Abyss.

It was a trap, you realize. Set by either Franklin Arnstadt or Lord Fear himself, the vault was a ruse in which to trap thieves long enough so that they might be found and taken to the dungeons, where they would be punished appropriately. You laugh silently at yourself. A thief as good as you, and you fell for an obvious trap like this.

Without realizing it, you lose track of time. Your life seems over, dragging on without end. How many days, or weeks, or years have you been lying here in this chamber of eight-legged horrors?

It may be decades later when a bright point of pain suddenly blossoms inside your head. You think that you are finally dying from the spiders' poisons. The room spins, howling with a churning, violent wind. You are suddenly dizzy, and your stomach clenches involuntarily. You close your eyes in pain.

The wind dies down, then disappears. Your stomach relaxes, and peace and cool air wash over you in a sweet breath. You look up, and you are in the audience chamber of King Halvor.

The king looks down at you from his throne. "Your spell has worked, cleric. They have been returned. But I do not see the crystal skull!" he announces angrily. "Your two days are up, thieves! What has happened?"

No one can answer him. The webs bind you so tightly, you cannot even move to signal for help.

The cleric rushes from his place on the dais and examines the three of you in turn, paying attention to the gray tint to your skin. Finally, he says, "Your Majesty, they have been subjected to a powerful spider venom, probably in a trap of Lord Fear's. They are paralyzed, my lord."

The king rubs his chin. "Can you do anything for them?"

"Yes, Your Majesty. If I may have but a few minutes in my chambers, I can concoct a mixture that will reverse the effects of the paralysis."

The king gestures for the cleric to hurry. You are left on the cold marble floor, your breast filled with a warm feeling of hope.

In ten minutes, the cleric returns with three cloths and a

bottle of a blue liquid. First, he carefully cuts the webbing away from your bodies with a sharp dagger. Then he pours the blue liquid onto a cloth, then places it over your mouth and nose. As he does the same for the others, your throat tingles with a cool, minty taste, and your lungs seem to shiver as the chemicals permeate your body.

Your eyes blink, and your skin feels as though it is being pricked with needles. Then you can move your fingers, and your arm, and in minutes the three of you are up on your feet, the paralysis gone. You bow before your king.

Go to 68.

5

The forest around you is cool and serene. High in the broad, leafy canopy above you, birds call out, chirping softly, and bright sunlight filters down through the leaves to dapple the winding path with golden freckles of light.

The peaceful woods of King Halvor surround his castle in a natural protective barrier. You follow the path to the edge of the forest, where it crosses a gravel road that stretches straight ahead to the castle.

You stop for a moment and stare at the proud towers reaching up into the blue, cloudless sky. Flags of all colors flap at the high pinnacles of the towers and turrets, and you can hear the hum of activity inside the castle walls, from the scores of people strolling and bartering in the market, filling the castle with the sounds of life. The castle stretches to each side in a fortress of brick and stone, and you can see curtains fluttering high in the windows of the keep, where the king and queen have their chambers.

The drawbridge is down this afternoon, as it always is until the setting of the sun, when darkness threatens the security of the realm. The gate to the castle is wide open. Two guards flank each side of the castle gate, and as you approach, one guard stares at you curiously.

You keep walking toward the drawbridge, and you try to swallow your fear. You have done nothing wrong—even if you are a professional thief—and these guards have no reason to suspect or accost you. Besides, it has been almost two months since you were last in King Halvor's realm, and surely it is safe for you to return. People, you are sure, have short memories, and no one now could possibly connect you with the missing emerald necklace of the Lady Carnassia.

Your footsteps echo hollowly as you step onto the drawbridge and start toward the gate. Then the sharp, shining blade of a spear is thrust in front of your face, and you suddenly stop short as the guard who has been watching you steps directly into your path.

"Now, what have we here?" the guard says.

Harveth, you remember, is this guard's name. He is one of the king's own handpicked guards, the Red Dragons ... and he certainly remembers you. From the day of the ball, you think.

"Excuse me?" you say innocently.

"Kir Trelander," he says, smirking behind his steel helmet. "I didn't think you'd ever have the courage to show your face around here again."

Harveth is about a foot taller than you, and the other guard is half a head taller than that. The idea of turning and running back to the safety of the forest flickers momentarily in your mind, but you decide to play this out for now. You can always run later.

"I had no idea my fame had spread so quickly through the realm. Trelander at your service," you say, bowing.

Harveth laughs. "Look here, Ygar," he says to the taller guard. "You were in training two months ago, but you've heard of the incident at the season's ball, have you not?"

"You mean the theft of the Lady Carnassia's necklace?"

Harveth laughed again. "More than that, Ygar. It was much bolder than that.

"King Halvor had gotten tired of the thieves and scoundrels skulking around the castle whenever the royal balls were held, when nobles and their ladies would wear their finest gold and jewels. The king passed an edict that security would be thrice as effective for the spring pageant, and the Dragons rounded up all the known thieves and rogues, all that we could find, and kept them safe and sound down in the comfortable confines of King Halvor's dungeon."

You chuckle ironically at that. The cool dungeon had been far from comfortable, and even though the king had kept the unofficial prisoners warm and happy with finer food than they could ever afford on their own, you had known it just wasn't right for a citizen to be imprisoned without just cause. The fear, alone, that a crime would be committed was not enough justification for imprisonment. You had done absolutely nothing illegal—though you had been planning to take advantage of the ball later that evening—and you had determined that you would make your point to the king.

Perhaps you did it too well.

"So, Shadow here," Harveth continues, "somehow talked one of the scullery workers, who was delivering the food to the prisoners, into parting with his uniform for a while—just long enough, it turned out, that Shadow got the chance to pass out delicacies to the nobles, pour wine for the queen herself, and surreptitiously steal seven money purses, two diamond bracelets, the famed Emerald Collar of the Lady Carnassia, right off her neck, and even the gold tooth of Lord Bleehall.

Ygar's mouth gapes open as he stares at you. "The gold tooth—"

Harveth smiles. "The lord, it seems, had a little too much mead that night and passed out at his table. While the Lady Pamelia danced away with nobles of the realm, Shadow, here, saw an opportunity for wealth."

Ygar's eyes seem to smolder at you. He doesn't like thieves, and he's ready to clap the irons across your wrists and haul you off to the dungeon. "What are we going to do with him?"

"Only some of that tale is true, Harveth," you say quickly, your eyes wide with innocence. "Indeed, I was rounded up, unjustly, with thieves and criminals from across the realm. But I had done nothing to warrant such treatment. I was totally innocent, and I would not put up with being confined with thieves and rabble. I merely seized the first opportunity to leave the dungeon and return to my home, which is exactly what I did.

"It was not I who stole into the royal ball, I can assure you. If it were, would I be standing here, talking with you today, risking my freedom? No, I suggest that it was another of the prisoners who also escaped, and then worked his way into the ball and stole away with the royals' finery. It was not I."

"He perfectly matched your description!" Harveth says angrily. "Height, weight, size..."

"If I remember correctly," you say carefully, "the thief was said to have much darker hair than mine, and he sported a thick moustache. You've seen me around the realm for a while, now—you were even the one who escorted me to the king's dungeon! Was my hair as dark as the culprit's? Did I have a moustache then?"

Harveth glowers at you. "No," he says, "your appearance was as it is now. But you could have had a disguise!"

You shake your head. "What thief carries a disguise around with him? No, this time, you've simply got the wrong man."

"I say take him in!" Ygar says. "Why take the chance?"

Harveth watches you, and a grin breaks out across his face. "No, we cannot take in a man simply on suspicion. We have to have proof before a suspect is brought on charges before the king. As to the ball, we have nothing but a few conflicting accounts. And besides," he says, smiling, "this thief has style."

He steps up and leans down into your face. "I cannot prove it was you, Shadow Trelander, who stole the emerald collar. I don't understand how you got away with it. But hear this: I know it was you, and you know it was

16 MICHAEL ANDREWS

you. You may pass into the castle today, maybe even tomorrow. But your crimes will catch up with you, and when they do, I'll be hauling you down to the dungeon permanently—and the food won't be half as good."

Harveth stands up and takes his position. "Now pass, citizen," he says officially. "Welcome to the castle of good King Halvor, and enjoy our lord's gracious hospitality. And remember, Shadow," he says, sneering, "I'm giving you just enough rope to hang yourself."

You thank the Forces for your good fortune today, and as you step quickly between the two guards, Harveth whispers to you, "By the way, the gold tooth was a nice touch."

Go to 62.

6

The effects of the sensory spell have worn off, and you are surrounded by Lord Fear's legions of the undead. Lord Fear himself stands before you in his long robes of black, a mist of darkness swirling at his feet.

He laughs at you again, then strides across the ballroom to an ornate chair. He sits and raises his hand. The undead rise stiffly to attention.

"This is now my home," Lord Fear says. His voice echoes hollowly across the room. "Come closer, little friends, so I may see your faces."

His eyes glow. He points at you with a clawed hand, and your body jerks toward him, uncontrollably, like a puppet.

The three of you stop a few paces from him, and Lord Fear releases you from his control. You sag, weakly, gasping for air. It was his eyes, you think. You can't let him look into your eyes, or he'll have you.

"I don't know how you found me here, but you have something of mine: the Crystal Skull of Sa'arkloth. Now, give it to me, or I shall have my servants take it from you by force."

"What skull?" you blurt out. "Do you see a skull anywhere on us?"

Keela looks at you with amazement in her eyes. Even Dare is proud you stood up to this evil thug.

Lord Fear stands. He towers above you, and you can feel the evil resonating from him. "Little man, you know nothing of the skull you have taken. Far more people across the world have been destroyed using the Skull of Sa'arkloth than you know. You think you have the strength to use it and live?"

Lord Fear grins mirthlessly. "No. Only I, among all the wizards of the ages, have been able to tap into its powers. Only I have been able to use it to siphon the energies of Arnstadt into myself. You dare to stand here and challenge me?"

You swallow and take a step back. "We—we just came here looking for easy pickings. We're thieves—all three of us—and we don't have any stinking skull of yours."

The thin smile on his face disappears. He sniffs in your direction, then points to your hip. "There, cur! I sense it on you, in that pouch of elven make. Now take it out, or my death knights shall slowly rip you apart and take it for me."

He gestures with an eyebrow, and the circle of undead warriors closes in a few feet. You look around nervously. Lord Fear has got you now.

You open the pouch. You reach inside, and your hand closes around the skull. Slowly, you pull the skull from the pouch—but you do not reveal the staff attached to it.

"You caught us," you say, jokingly. "Is this the skull you wanted? You know, I thought I saw another skull just like this down there—"

"There is no other skull like this." Lord Fear hisses angrily. "Now hand it to me, boy."

You move toward him. "This old thing is what you want? All right."

You hold it out, waiting. Lord Fear steps away from the throne, his hands outstretched.

And you toss it away behind you, sliding it across the floor. The undead warriors stare blankly at their master, awaiting his command. Their dead, unholy eyes never notice the skull and pouch sliding across the floor, between their legs.

Lord Fear steps toward you, anger making his gray face turn blood red. "Kill them, warriors! Kill them and feast on their bones!"

The undead stir. Their eyes blaze with smoldering fires, and they approach. Simultaneously, the three of you bring up your swords in defense. "I hope you've got a plan," Keela says.

"Not much of one," you tell her. "Just make sure you don't look into his eyes."

Then the undead are upon you, and you tear into them

like a berserker. Never have you fought like this before. You are filled with rage at the evil and the injustice this foul being has caused. How many deaths must you put up with? How much longer will he go on tormenting the people of the realm?

No, it is up to you to stop him here and now, before his evil influence spreads across the world.

The undead fall away from you and the onslaught of your blade, and you make your way slowly toward the skull. Near you, Dare cuts a wide swath through the slow-moving fighters, and Keela holds her own, ducking and parrying away from the undead, and tearing into them when they do not expect it.

You pause. The undead around you stop momentarily, and you look to your friends, wondering what is happening. Then your mouth gapes in shock, for Dare is staring at Lord Fear. The black wizard's hand is gesturing wildly, and you can see that he has taken Dare under his hypnotic spell.

Dare starts walking toward the crystal skull, to take it back to his new master.

"No!" you scream. "Noooo!"

Dare lifts the skull and pouch in his hands. In terror, you momentarily forget your battle, and the death knights surround you in force. You are swamped under their sheer numbers. One undead fighter rips the sword from your hand and tosses it away. You hear it clatter to the floor, then you are defenseless.

Their cold hands grip you tightly. Above the melee, you hear Lord Fear say coldly, "Bring them here."

The fight is over. The death knights hold you and Keela in their clammy grasp, and you are brought before their liege as an offering.

You look down. Dare presents the skull and pouch and places them at Lord Fear's feet . . .

. . . right next to your sword, unnoticed at the feet of an undead fighter.

Fear steps away from the throne. Dare is grabbed by the

undead as Fear's control fades away. "How delicious," Fear says. "Betrayed by one of your own. Now, little ones, you shall taste my power. Now you shall taste my wrath. Witness the power of the Crystal Skull . . . the Crystal Skull of Fear."

This is it, you realize. The undead are all watching Lord Fear, and you are sure you can twist out of their grasp for one last move.

Both the skull and sword are right in front of you. The skull, you know, will destroy Lord Fear. But you don't know how to use it.

On the other hand, you certainly know how to use a good sword. But can Lord Fear be stopped by sharpened steel alone?

Lord Fear smiles and reaches down for the crystal skull.

If you leap for the skull, go to 65.

If you leap for the sword, go to 17.

7

You have no idea what dangers lurk in the dark woods surrounding Carnivex Mansion, so you quickly decide to escape the undead warriors that are chasing you by taking the old road you followed to get here.

You gather the reins of your mount and shout, "Ho!" then point toward the front of the mansion. Your companions follow suit, and the three horses start off at a furious gallop away from the ragged line of undead warriors dropping from the window.

You round the corner of the mansion, and Bentley snorts in abject terror, digging trenches in the earth with his hooves as he braces himself to a stop. The others pound closer behind you, then halt abruptly as their horses scent the newly risen dead.

The earth in front of Carnivex Mansion is full of holes,

each surrounded by piles of earth where the undead have dug themselves out of their shallow graves.

They stand there, fifty of them, all undead servants of your nemesis, Lord Fear; all moist with the dank richness of soil as it drops from them in clods; all staring at you with hungry flames in their soulless eyes.

"By the Forces!" Dare cries, unsheathing his shining broadsword from its scabbard.

Your horse rears up, and you feel as though you are about to fall. But you steady your steed and turn him back toward the forest, where a safe haven from the undead awaits. But you are too late, for countless soldiers of Lord Fear have crept up on you from behind, and you are surrounded by a legion of the undead.

Then they attack. They pull down your horses first, then scramble for you with their clenching claws of exposed bone and rotting flesh. You see Keela disappear as they swarm over her, then Dare, still hacking at them with his shining blade, is pulled to the ground and buried under their chomping teeth.

You attempt to scurry away, diving between legs of pale bone and purplish, pulsing muscle, then your arms are grasped tightly in a cold, steely clench, and you are jerked roughly to the ground.

They are upon you. You feel their unyielding, freezing, sharpened teeth sink deep into your flesh, and your vision seems to swim sluggishly, blurring with grayness and fog. All you feel is cold—the numbing, eternal cold of the grave. You no longer recoil with terror at the touch of the undead. Soon, you feel nothing, and as you look up at the stars swirling endlessly, so high up in the night sky, you dimly consider that you will soon come to understand what endless really means.

* * * * *

And you are right.
When next you open your eyes, the night is alive with

light. Animals that scamper about on the ground seem to pulsate with an energy that calls to you, makes you drool with hunger.

You move toward the animal, a rabbit, but it senses you and rushes away in terror, and your meal is gone.

You turn. There, somewhere in the mountains, you sense a large gathering of food, of pulsating energy.

A city of humans . . .

For that energy is life, and as you are now one of the legions of the undead, your only purpose is to feed off the living . . . and heed the voice of he who commands you . . .

Lord Fear.

Welcome to the endless night.

The End

8

You do not know who stole the crystal skull, but surely it is a valuable item, almost priceless. Any thief worth his merit would run with the skull as far as he could go . . . or get rid of it now and make a quick, handsome profit. To do that, he would go to a black marketeer—a "fence." You know all the fences of the realm, having done business with most of them in the past. But if you were the thief of the crystal skull, you would take it to a fence who knows the value of such a rare item. You would take it to the most appraising fence in the realm. You smile, thinking of only one man any accomplished thief would go to: the most infamous fence of the realm. His stall is located here in the bazaar, and he trades honestly as both a healer and an antiquities dealer.

You look at Keela. Simultaneously, you both say, "Charnom."

"What?" the cleric asks.

"Nothing," you say, hoping you did not unwittingly reveal the fence's name to the cleric. "We must go, the three of us," you tell him, indicating Keela and Dare. "This is our quest, not yours. We will begin our search outside. We shall return when we are ready, and have no fear, cleric, we will find the skull and return it to the king."

The cleric nods and motions for a guard. Together, your band is led through the castle to the front entrance. You pass through the doors and blink at the bright sunlight reflecting off the colorful tents and signs of the marketplace.

"Where are we going?" Dare asks.

"We are going to see a man about a skull," you say.

"I don't know. Are you sure we shouldn't have inspected the treasury first? I mean, who out here would know anything about the crystal skull?"

You shake your head. Warriors can be so dense at times. Look," you tell him, "if a thief steals something that is valuable, then he usually tries to sell it and make a profit, right?"

Dare tries to understand. "But who in the bazaar is so dishonest that they would buy something that they know has been stolen from their king?"

This warrior is so naive. "There is always a market for strange, one-of-a-kind items. Stolen items, magical items—it does not matter. It is called the black market, and we're going to see the most knowledgeable black marketeer that I know."

"Charnom," Keela says. "He knows more about antiquities and curios than anyone. If the skull has been stolen by a thief, then he certainly knows about it."

You make your way through the bazaar, pushing through to the back of the market, arranged along the west wall of the castle. Here the most established merchants long ago set up permanent tents or staked out alcoves or cubbyholes in the castle wall. In the far corner of the walls, in an alley between a corner tower and an adjacent building, you come to the scarlet tent of Charnom, the merchant.

On tables and along the ground, brass and silver trinkets gleam in the sun. Fabrics from the south, woven with gold, are arranged in bolts on one table, and from the shadows of the alley you hear a boisterous voice shout "Shadow! Shadow! It has been too long! Come in! Talk with an old man for a while! Come in, come in!"

The three of you bend down and pass underneath the table. The air in the alley is still, much cooler than out in the sunlight, and tables arranged along the walls are covered with goblets and swords from the east, jewelry forged in the west, and shining, priceless items stolen from the vaults and jewelry boxes of the lords and ladies of all the realm.

The voice speaks again from the darkness of the alley. "Finally come out of hiding, eh? About time, young man. Now, where's that emerald collar you not so quietly stole? I'll give you a good price for it, you know."

The old man appears from around a sheet hung across the alley. His head is bald, save for a fringe of white running from temple to temple, and his eyes seem to gleam with good humor.

The two of you embrace, for at times Charnom has been like a father to you. He knows Keela, of course, so you introduce him to Dare, and then tell him that the three of you must talk. "Of course," you say, looking from Charnom to Dare, "everything we say will be kept private. No confidences will be broken by any of us."

Charnom nods. He knows that Dare is a servant of the king, and he waits for a response.

Dare scowls. If this man is a criminal, then the king should know about it. But Dare has been charged by the king with a quest to find the skull. If dealing with this black marketeer will lead them to it, then he will do as he is asked.

Dare nods. "Agreed."

Charnom leads you behind the sheet, where you take a seat upon piles of old cushions that he has arranged for visitors. Here, in the alley, you can speak in privacy. "The Crystal Skull of Sa'arkloth," you say to Charnom. "What do you know about it?"

The old man's eyes grow wide. He makes a frantic symbol with the fingers of his right hand to ward off evil. "It is an accursed object!" Charnom says vehemently. "It is said to have been crafted by the undead, and cursed by the Forces as an abomination! Legend has it that it was finally destroyed in the Valley of Stars, thrown back into the smoldering crater where the uncarved crystal had first been found. Other than this, I know nothing, except I should have nothing to do with it, ever!" His face wrinkles into an expression of curiosity. "Why do you come to me? You should go instead to a wizard or scholar."

"Yes," you say, "but you believe too much in old legends." You move closer to him and speak softly. "The crystal skull still exists. Up until recently, it was hoarded in the treasury of King Halvor himself."

Charnom gasps. "Here?"

You nod. "And now the treasury has been broken into,

and the skull has been stolen." You place your hand on his arm. "We need your help, Charnom. It is our duty to return the skull to the king, and so we must find the thief who took it."

You quickly explain the situation to Charnom, who listens thoughtfully to every word.

You finish your tale, and he leans toward you. "Now I understand. You think that some thief has brought it to me to be, well . . . disposed of." He shakes his head, his eyes blazing. "I would have nothing to do with such a thing as that. If someone brought it to me, I would send him away with the thing burning a hole of evil through his heart. It is a cursed thing, the Skull of Sa'arkloth. No, no one has come to me with the skull. I did not even know it still existed. And I wish I did not now."

You sit back against the wall and think. Charnom was your only lead, and you have no idea where to turn next for help.

Finally, the old man says, "I keep my ears open for all information of this type." He places a hand on your arm. "I have heard nothing about the crystal skull, my friend. And you know that if the skull were truly on the black market, I would have heard something about it."

You smile. Charnom is right. He knows everything that goes on in the bazaar.

"No," Charnom says, "I think you must retrace your steps. I do not believe a professional thief took the skull, for I would have heard even a whisper of information concerning its theft. Something else is going on here. You should return to the keep and ask to examine the vault. Who knows what clues the perpetrators have left behind?"

You nod. You should have thought of that earlier.

The three of you stand and make your leave. You embrace Charnom again and promise you'll come around again to see him—if you can bring back the skull, that is.

You return to the palace. Dare leads you back to the hall where the king is attending to the business of the realm. The cleric is still with him. They both watch you approach.

Go to 57.

9

"Wait!" you shout at the guards. "Wait!"

They turn abruptly, pulling their broadswords from the scabbards at their belts. "Stand clear!" the huge guard orders you, pointing his sharp sword at your chest. "Do not interfere with our duties!"

"No! You don't understand!" You stop a few feet from the captain of the guard and hold up your hands. "I am unarmed," you say. "And you may as well take me in, too."

The captain scowls angrily at you. His face is bright red with anger. "Is this some kind of a trick?" he asks, gruffly.

You look into the eyes of Keela, and you think you see a glimmer of gratitude in her expression. Calmly, surely, you say, "No, no trick, Captain. But I am with her. And I'm the one you should be looking for, not her. I'm Shadow."

Keela sighs, held in the guards' strong grip. They all stare at you. The captain takes a step closer and looks you up and down. "Shadow . . ." he says. "Yes, I recognize you now, even without your paltry disguise." He grabs you roughly and throws you facefirst into the dirt of the castle grounds. You taste the grit between your teeth as the captain clamps two heavy iron shackles around your wrists. You feel the stares of people in the marketplace as you lie helplessly at the mercy of the Red Dragons. Then the captain hauls you up to your feet, and he shoves you together with Keela.

She looks into your eyes. "You didn't have to come back for me," she says.

"Well, we're in this together, aren't we? 'Honor among

thieves,' right? Besides, you would have done the same for me."

"We're untrustworthy. We're thieves." She grins. "Don't count on it."

You laugh, knowing full well that if the tables had been turned, you could have counted on her to come to your aid—or, at least, stick by your side.

You are shoved in the back, and another guard shoves Keela. "Get a move on!" the captain bellows, pushing you toward the keep. "There used to be a price on your head, thief, and a substantial reward for the emerald collar. I'll look right good to the king for bringing in the criminal of the year."

You whisper to Keela, "The only thing that will make him look good is a sack over his head."

She laughs, and it makes you feel good that you didn't turn your back on her. The ugly guard shoves you again. "Keep moving," he says, "quickly! You've both got an appointment with the king!"

Go to 72.

10

When you get close, you notice that the door is slightly ajar. The three of you step back with your weapons at the ready, prepared for an attack from within. Dare creeps up to the door, then slams it open with a mighty kick.

Hazy sunlight filters in through a shattered window at the rear of the room. Cabinets hang open along one wall, empty save for dust and spiderwebs. A long, massive table lies angled across the floor, and several chairs lie shattered into spindly shards nearby. All over the floor, the sharp remains of glasses, ancestral plates, and stoneware lie cracked and smashed, littering the floor like broken eggshells.

You step gingerly through the destruction in the dining

room, careful of the sharp edges on the shattered plates, and the three of you search the room from wall to wall. Dare helps you pull the cabinets away from the wall, but nothing lies behind them.

"Nothing here," Keela says. "Let's try another room before it gets too late."

Go to 25.

11

You pause to consider your dream. The dream bird had the ring in its beak, just like the carved stone bird above the crypt's door. But the bird dropped the ring, and the lion took it, dragging it in a line across the floor.

Pulling it in a line . . .

"I think I know what my dream meant. Let's pull the lion's ring."

You reach up and grasp the black iron ring with both hands. You tense your muscles, then pull.

The ring does not budge.

You motion the warrior over, and he takes the ring in his huge hands and braces one foot against the wall.

His muscles stand out with the strain. Then his hands pull the ring away from the wall, pulling a thick black cord of steel behind it in a line.

Mechanisms spin behind the wall as the ring is released and slowly inches back into the lion's mouth. A door opens on hidden hinges at the base of the wall—one of the burial markers is false—and a secret opening is revealed that is large enough for a man to enter.

Inside, the witchlight floats above three ancient sarcophagi. In one corner, a wooden casket lies on the floor, tightly bound with thick iron chains and rusted padlocks.

You blow dust off the top of the closest sarcophagus and read the name of Franklin Arnstadt. Beside that are the resting places of Arnstadt's beloved wife, Angeline,

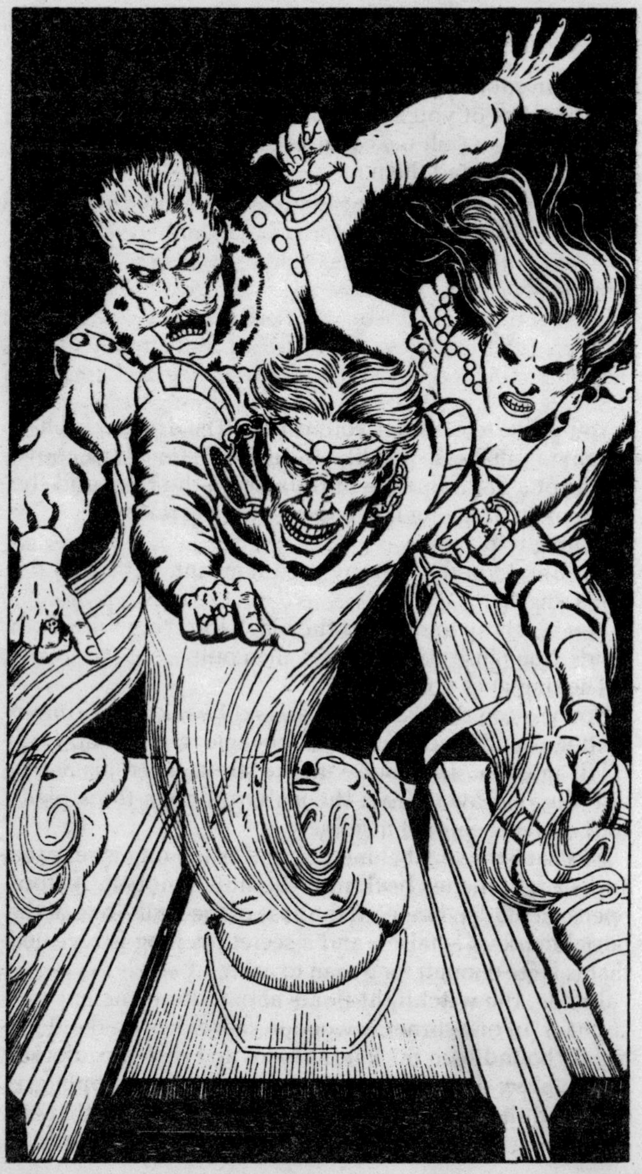

and his brother, Bretski.

The light weaves playfully among the three of you, then passes harmlessly into each sarcophagus and returns to float above the floor. The air in the secret room grows deathly cold. Your breath comes out in white clouds, and the witchlight flickers violently, like lightning.

Three translucent shapes begin to form in the cold, still air, hanging like mist above their sarcophagi. The restless ghosts of the original Arnstadts hover before you, dressed in their funereal attire. Each spirit points to one of you, and their voices echo together like an ancient chant, gradually rising in pitch like the howl of an unnatural wind.

The ancestral land of the Arnstadts has been tainted by foulness. The souls of Arnstadt are in scarlet limbo and cry out for deliverance. You have received our message and trusted in our messenger. Now we can do nothing but trust in you.

Three things we must tell you, wanderers, three things you must remember if our land is to be saved:

That which you seek is deeply hidden upon a pedestal of power.

That which you must defeat can be overcome by the two that once were one.

The scarlet prisoners can be freed in the risen light.

Remember these things well, paladins. Seek not to disturb these bones, or cursed be ye. Seek the corrupt one in our ancestral home, and find your path before the foul one rises in power.

You are the land's only hope.

The ghosts fold their wrists upon their chests and bow their heads. Together they fade away, and silence hangs in the chill air. The blue light hovers above the sarcophagi, flickering softly.

You are the first to speak. "So that is what my dream was—a call from the spirits for help."

"And the light is their messenger, sent to bring us here," Keela says.

Dare grunts. "I like none of this. Spirits and evil! Let us get out of here and prepare to search the castle."

You nod. "I agree. We've got a few more hours we can

rest, then we can leave for the castle with the morning light."

"What about these coffins?" the thief asks. "These people were royalty. They were probably buried with all their precious, ancestral jewels." She points to the corner. "Look at that one! There has to be a reason it's chained up like that. Maybe that's where all the jewels are."

You shake your head. "Remember what the spirits said? 'Seek not to disturb these bones, or cursed be ye.'"

"Curses!" Dare says. "I am fed up with ghosts and curses and the undead. I want something I can touch with my bare steel! I want action!"

"I say we open the coffins," Keela says. "We'll regret it if we don't."

You say, "What if we regret it if we do?"

If you open a sarcophagus, go to 44.

If you break open the chained coffin, go to 38.

If you return to the Red Room Inn, go to 3.

12

When you awake, the sun is coming over the mountains in the distance. It is the morning of the second day of your quest, and you are ready to get this over with and return to the bosom of the king's realm.

The three of you prepare a light breakfast, then ride your horses toward Castle Arnstadt, where you believe Lord Fear is holing up with his armies.

You ride for more than half an hour, then stop at a deep chasm, which forms a natural moat. The river rushes far below a bridge that leads to Castle Arnstadt, situated high upon a cliff.

The three of you stare at the castle, for you can tell that Lord Fear's unnatural evil has tainted the land and corrupted the very citadel that he has stolen.

Where once proud towers stood, now the stones and bricks are overgrown with black vines and foul mold. The sky above is ashen, somehow blocking the sunlight, and the grass and trees around the castle are withered and black, dying slowly from the lord's evil.

Castle Arnstadt has been transformed into Castle Fear.

You swallow nervously. No, you do not want to go in there. You can feel Lord Fear's cold evil from here. But you steel yourself and urge your horse forward anyway. You've come too far to give up now.

The bridge leads directly into the castle. The portcullis is wide open, as though Lord Fear is ignorant that anyone is after him—or so sure of himself that he believes he can defeat any enemy.

The closer you get to the cylindrical tower that is the keep, the harder it is to breathe. You are inhaling the cold essence of his evil, you realize, and something within you rebels at evil's very scent.

"It is not too late," you say without thinking. The others look at you as though they were thinking the same thing. "I mean, we know Lord Fear is here. We can sense him." The others nod. "We can return to King Halvor now and get reinforcements. Lord Fear isn't going anywhere."

"But what about the skull?" the thief says. "We don't know for sure that he has it."

You consider that. All indications are that Fear does have the crystal skull. But if the king comes to conquer Lord Fear and doesn't get the skull back, then he'll come running to you and put you in his dungeon.

Some days, it seems like you just can't win. What are you going to do?

If you enter the castle, go to 28.

If you return to the king, go to 15.

13

"Wait," you tell the others.

Dare looks at you from atop his steed. "Come, Shadow. I want to return to the warmth of my home. This village is home only to the dead."

"That's just it," you say. "I think . . ." You pause, unsure of yourself, but you have to check it out. "I don't think the villagers are really dead."

You open your magical pouch and reach inside. You bring out your hand and hold up one of the scarlet gems you took from Lord Fear's vault. Almost vibrating with an inner life, it hums in your palm.

You take it between your thumb and forefinger and peer closer. The ruby contains absolutely no flaws, and you are right—you can feel it thrumming with power, almost like a pulse.

Then you hear Keela cry out, "Shadow! Look!"

The rays of the sun are cresting the Forest of Shades. They feel warm on your arm and hand, and the gem sparkles with sunlight. Keela points to beside you. You turn and stare.

The rays of sunlight angling through the ruby create a rainbow on the ground. But you are not staring at a band of colors: you are staring at the perfect image of a woman, cast by the sunlight filtering through the scarlet gem.

It comes to you in a rush. You know what to do instinctively, but the others stare at you, dumbfounded.

"The clues! The clues told us all we needed to know. 'The scarlet prisoners can be freed in the risen light.' That's what the ghosts said!"

You take a handful of the rubies from your pouch. The sun is a brilliant ball of fire just above the horizon, and you toss the gems into the sky to be graced by the golden light.

The air around you seems to sing as you take the pouch and scatter the gems to the wind. The song rises to a high-pitched song of life and redemption, and on the searing rays of the sun, the gems shatter into scarlet dust and are whirled throughout the village upon the winds.

Around you, the odd-looking trees come to life. Twisting, reaching, their bark withers away and changes color, becoming pale and soft, like flesh. Branches become hands; twigs become fingers. Roots are transformed back into feet.

You shout with joy. The scarlet gems had been the souls of the villagers, who had been transformed by Lord Fear, using the powers of the crystal skull, in order to hoard them and feed on the gems' latent energies. What Lord Fear had left were lifeless husks, strange, gnarled trees that no one would suspect were the bodies of the villagers.

The people of the village transform back to their normal selves. The Red Room door opens, and a small, burly man walks out—the little tree behind the bar had been the dwarven innkeeper. As one, the villagers look at the sun, and then the three of you, and they thank you for restoring them to life.

The story of Lord Fear's coming to Arnstadt is revealed to you: how he came at sunset with his unliving army, how he attacked the village in one single instant, transforming villagers where they walked in the streets or ate in their homes. His legions of undead collected the gems, then they stormed Castle Arnstadt and brought darkness to their village, recreating the castle in Fear's own design.

In the light of morning, you look toward the castle. There, you are sure, the current head of the Arnstadt family has been restored, for the castle itself gleams brightly and the taints of evil and darkness that had corrupted the castle are gone.

You jump upon your horse and make your good-byes. The journey back to the realm lies before you, and you have an appointment with the king—to prove your innocence and return to him the Crystal Skull of Sa'arkloth.

Go to 70.

14

Keela slaps the guard with the palm of her hand, but he is so huge and burly that he laughs it off as though it were nothing. "A mosquito sting, little thief," the guard says. "Ha! You'll have to do better than that."

"Just give me a chance!" Keela cries, but the guard grabs her arms and easily passes her on to the other guards behind him.

He looks you over, trying to decide just what you were up to with the thief. "And who might you be?" the guard says.

You look in Keela's eyes, wide with fear of her captors. You could try to help her somehow, but all you can think about is being taken before the king yourself, and being sentenced to the dungeon—or worse—for your pranks at the royal ball.

It is hard to speak, and you cannot look Keela in her eyes, but you believe you have no other choice at this point, for is not discretion the better part of valor?

"I am just a citizen, guard," you say. "This woman approached me and asked me to buy her a drink. Then you entered and captured her. So she's a thief, eh? I guess I'm lucky she didn't try to rob me."

The guard nods slowly, as if he is judging your words and your appearance. Apparently, what you said convinced him, and he doesn't recognize you at all. "I'm sure she would have robbed you eventually, sir," he says. "You can't trust a lowlife thief like this one. I've got no idea what the king might want with a thief, but you'd be well advised to stay away from the likes of her."

You swallow uneasily. "Thank you, guardsman. I'll remember your advice."

Keela stares at you silently with an expression of horrified surprise on her face. Then she starts kicking and yelling against her captors, and they drag her into the street. You hear her call your name once, angrily, then all three guards carry her toward the palace.

She disappears from view, and you slowly sit back in your chair. The patrons in the tavern are watching you, and when you face their stares, they look away, as though they are embarrassed to be in the same room with you.

Your face grows hot with shame. *I didn't want to do that,* you think, *but what choice did I have? I would have gone to trial for the night of the ball—and I couldn't let myself be caught.*

The serving woman comes over. She takes your glass off the table and looks down at you scornfully. "Nash says you have to leave. He doesn't want your kind in here."

Your mouth hangs open. "What did I do?" you stammer.

"He doesn't serve cowards in here," Jaan says. "He refuses to serve anybody who would do that to a friend."

You find that you have no reply to that. You stand slowly, feeling all the stares on you as you trudge toward the door. You pause with your hand on the doorknob, and you look back only once. Nash, the bartender, is standing with his arms crossed, watching you. "And don't come back," he says, and he turns away to clean a mug.

Outside, the sunlight does little to dispel the dark shame you have brought to yourself. You see Keela being led toward the castle, a guard at each side. You still have time to act; however, the gate leading to the outside—and to safety—is still close by.

If you go to help Keela, go to 9.

If you leave the castle, go to 33.

15

You stare at the depressing monument to evil that Castle Arnstadt has been transformed into, and you shiver with terror. No, you do not want to face Lord Fear in this bleak place; better to ride back to the king, return with reinforcements, and defeat Lord Fear and his armies with the soldiers of the realm.

The others agree when you tell them your plan, and together you ride at a furious gallop away from the castle and the village of Arnstadt. The Forest of Shades is a dark green blur as you hasten your horse on as fast as you can over the rough ground. At about noon you come to Carnivex Mansion and spur your horse on to a greater speed down the old country road, back into the realm of King Halvor.

Shortly before nightfall, the guards allow you entrance to the castle. Your horses are taken by the stablemaster for proper care, and you are escorted into the audience chamber of the king.

"So soon?" he cries when he sees you. "Already, you return to me with the Crystal Skull of Sa'arkloth?"

The three of you kneel and bow your heads. "No, Your Majesty," the warrior says. "The crystal skull is beyond our reach. Lord Fear has conquered the village of Arnstadt in the northern provinces. He has raised armies of the dead, and has taken the ancestral castle of Arnstadt as his own.

"Lord Fear has the skull, my lord. With it, we believe, he has increased his powers tremendously, and he is probably the cause of all the villagers disappearing.

"We returned for reinforcements, Your Majesty. We are no match for a legion of Lord Fear's walking dead, and we believe we need the royal army to conquer Lord Fear and return the skull to you."

The king asks for more of an explanation, and the three of you alternate telling the story of your journey. The king and his cleric are horribly dismayed by the disappearance of the villagers and Lord Fear's powers over the undead, and they ask you many questions concerning the evil lord's might.

Then the king is silent for a long time. He finally gazes at you and allows himself a smile. "The realm thanks you all for your service to the king. But what you have told us casts a shadow upon us all.

"Shadow, you and Keela are free to go. Although you were not successful in your quest, you return to us with honor, and with a warning of Lord Fear's evil. The realm is indebted to you.

"We now have no recourse but to conquer Lord Fear and regain the crystal skull, for with its powers, Fear can overthrow the entire world." The king snaps his fingers. "Vizier!" The royal vizier appears as if from nowhere. "Inform the army: We ride into battle before the next light. We ride to conquer Lord Fear and his evil! Tell them to prepare well, for our enemy commands an army of the undead.

"Go now, and gather all the clerics and mages we have in our service. We shall have need of them in the heat of battle."

The vizier runs off to spread the word of the king. The king rises and places a hand on your shoulder. "Go now, thieves. The horses that brought you back are yours to keep. Go in peace, and know that you have the thanks of your king."

You bow in honor to King Halvor, and you and Keela leave the king's chamber. Unescorted by the king's guards, you lead Keela through the halls of the castle until you come to an alcove where a long mahogany armoire stands. You casually glance around for onlookers, then, spying no one, you reach behind the armoire and pluck out a large leather pouch. You stuff it in your tunic and hurry away.

"What is that?" Keela asks.

"Outside. You'll see."

Outside, the two horses, gifts from the king, await you. You ride them quickly through the gates, then slow to a trot on the road leading to the thief's home village.

You take the pouch out of your tunic and open it for her. Moonlight gleams like jade fire inside the large emerald and glints with starlight off the polished gold.

"The emerald collar!" Keela says.

You laugh. "I never had it. I hid it right under the king's nose the night it was stolen. Now . . ." You pause. "Perhaps the theft can come to some good in the village of Arnstadt. If the king defeats Lord Fear and returns the villagers, then they will need all the help they can get."

Keela looks at you with admiration. Together, the two of you ride off to await the news from Arnstadt, and to perhaps return there with kindness and caring as your gifts.

* * * * *

At dawn of the next day, five hundred of the king's warriors and a score of the realm's magic-users rode forth do do battle with the undead forces of Lord Fear.

Galloping hard across the land, the forces were able to arrive at Arnstadt in the afternoon. After a short period for reconnaissance and to prepare for a siege, the armies of King Halvor attacked Castle Fear with all their might.

Caught unaware, the undead fighters were destroyed easily and Lord Fear was defeated and ridded of his powers by the realm's mages. Incarcerated in the king's dungeons within powerful spells of imprisonment, Nevill Carnivex's pleas to the dark forces went unanswered, and in time the former Lord Fear became nothing but the lord of his own twisted, labyrinthine fantasies of revenge.

The Crystal Skull of Sa'arkloth was discovered in a hidden vault under the dungeon of Lord Fear, and with its magical powers, the wizards of the realm were able to return the villagers of Arnstadt to life.

But the villagers returned to find their homes in ruin, their businesses all but destroyed. If it were not for the generous, anonymous donation of a priceless emerald necklace, the village would have been abandoned. As it is, the gift brought enough money to repair all the buildings of the village, and brought food and warmth to all.

You are a hero.

The End

16

You try to fight off the sleepiness that has come over you, but what is the point? This room is so inviting, nothing could possibly hurt you here, right?

The bed is so soft, so perfectly comfortable, that you are heedless of the dust that spreads over you. You snuggle under the blankets and smile, thinking of the portrait's—Angeline's—eyes, and how beautiful she is, how loving, how easy it would be to drown in her kisses. . . .

You see her then, laughing and dancing with her husband, Franklin Arnstadt, in the glorious ballroom downstairs. Part of you knows this is a dream; the other part dimly realizes that what you are dreaming is something that took place long in the past. This is Angeline's tale—you saw her ghost in the Arnstadt crypt—and you are nothing but a silent witness to the events of the forgotten past. . . .

The most beautiful woman in all the realm, she dances with grace and ease. All the people of the realm love her, and none more so than her husband, dashing Franklin. But a foul sorceress, jealous of the affection bestowed on the woman by the populace, places Angeline under a curse during the spring ball.

It is there that Bretski, Franklin's brother, is bewitched and forces a duel—a duel for the beauteous Angeline. Franklin understands nothing of his brother's actions and tries to reason with him. Under the sorceress's spell, Bretski attacks, and the brothers clash swords in a furious battle that spills out of the ballroom and into the hall.

It is there that Angeline pleads for sanity.

It is there that Angeline pleads for a return of peace.

It is there that Bretski knocks the blade from his brother's hand, and raises his sword to deliver the death blow.

It is there that Angeline throws herself in front of her beloved husband and begs Bretski to stop this duel.

And it is there that Bretski's sword comes down, unstoppably, and kills the beautiful Angeline with a single, misspent thrust.

The realm weeps at Angeline's loss. The brother, despondent over actions he had no control of, throws himself upon his own sword. Franklin, in mourning for his family, finally uncovers the truth, and the sorceress is stripped of her powers by the local mages, and is placed in a dismal dungeon for the rest of her life.

You rise out of your dream slowly, as though you are in a fog. The room is swimming in mist, swirling like the boundaries between the realms of reality and dreams. You are sleepy still, and yearn to fall back into night's sweet embrace.

But you see her eyes, looking at you, and you long for her embrace.

The mists part, and Angeline steps from them. Her long gown flows with swirling smoke, and, floating across the room to hover above the bed, she reaches for you. Her lips, full and red, are above yours. and her soft hair curls around you like a thing alive.

You purse your lips for a long, endless embrace with your fantasy love.

The ghost of Angeline Arnstadt, doomed to forever walk the earth in search of her true love, takes you in her arms.

"Franklinnnn . . ." she whispers, her cool lips pressing against yours.

And you know love . . .

* * * * *

Much later, it seems, you awake. Angeline is there, more beautiful than you could ever imagine.

She is radiant, glowing with life, and she calls to you, beckoning you to her.

Then she takes your hand. Franklin appears, and Bretski, and they gesture for you to join them.

The castle now is forever yours. Together, the souls of

the doomed will haunt the Arnstadt castle for eternity.

Such is the price of a kiss from the dead.

The End

17

You want the skull badly, but its powers are unknown to you, and in the few seconds you have before Lord Fear's hand wraps around the skull, you conclude that your only hope is your sword.

It lies only inches from you. You can already feel it in your hand.

With a mighty heave, you wrench yourself from the grip of the death knights. You take one leap, and your hand closes around the hilt of your sword.

You bring it up, the fires of justice burning fiercely in your heart.

Lord Fear stands frozen, watching you, his hand reaching for the skull.

With one powerful lunge, you drive your sword straight through Lord Fear. The bloodless blade protrudes from his back, and Fear looks down at you, not unkindly, but with black humor.

He laughs, like a bark, and he pulls the sword from his body as though it were nothing but a splinter. It comes to you then, the ghosts' warning: 'That which you must defeat can be overcome by the two that were once one' . . . the skull and the staff.

Lord Fear laughs and laughs, and as his undead warriors hold you tightly, he takes the skull in his hands and jerks away your magic pouch. "Complete," he says. "You have remade the Staff of Sa'arkloth. I am indebted to you, sir," he says, bowing. "The skull and staff have not been complete for centuries, and now my dominion over the earth shall be tripled. For bringing it to me, your reward shall be a quick, painless death."

The room fills with the echoes of Fear's scratchy laughter. Then he approaches you with your own sword.

His thrust is fast. You barely feel the steel penetrate your heart.

You welcome the peaceful darkness.

* * * * *

When you awaken, it is to do the bidding of your master. You do not notice your friends silently serving King Fear. You notice nothing but the wishes of your king, and his orders for you.

If you were aware of anything, you would be aware that your death was quick and relatively painless, as Fear promised. But Lord Fear never said anything about your undeath. . . .

And in undeath, you belong to King Fear.

For if you were aware, you would see that with the completed skull and staff, which you so naively let fall into his hands, Lord Fear quickly conquered the realm of King Halvor, then went on to claim the continent. In less than a year, the world belonged to Lord Fear, who claimed himself king, and let darkness play upon the face of the earth, and turned humanity into toys for the powers of evil.

But you notice nothing . . . nothing but the voice of your dark-dwelling master and the unholy blaze in his eyes.

The End

18

No, you cannot leave something so obviously valuable as these scarlet gems in a death trap like this. You open your new pouch and see the staff you found in Carnivex Mansion. You pull it out of the bottomless pouch and place it on the floor, then you start scooping the gems inside. You look at Keela and hold out your hand, filled with little rubies. "You want some?"

She shakes her head violently. "I don't want anything from this foul place. I just want to get out alive."

The hundreds of gems are secure in your pouch. You tie the golden drawstring tight, then pat the pouch to be sure. It feels as though there is hardly anything in it.

"Now what do we do?" Keela asks.

You place your hands on your hips and glare at the crystal skull. It is protected by a spell of blind energy around the obsidian pedestal, and you have no way to grab the skull and run. If only you had something with which to push it off the pedestal. Then Dare could catch it, and you could get out long before darkness falls and Lord Fear discovers the theft.

You look around for something long enough to reach into the pedestal's range of power. Then you glance at your feet and notice the ornate staff you found in Carnivex Mansion. It looks long enough and sturdy enough to you so that . . .

And then you understand.

Go to 34.

19

"Where?" the female thief asks.

You slowly spin on your heels. Your eyes finally settle on the long oaken staircases at each side of the front doors, leading up to a shadow-shrouded gallery, and from there . . . to who knows where?

"There," you say suddenly. "Upstairs, in the other rooms."

Dare looks up and follows your gaze. "There are probably only bedrooms up there," he says, confused. "Why would Lord Fear hide something as valuable as the crystal skull up in a simple bedroom?"

The female thief tries to stifle a laugh. "Because simple

people would never suspect a valuable item to be hidden in plain sight," she says.

Dare rubs his chin, contemplating the strategy. "Hmm."

You shake your head as the thief smiles knowingly at you. "Upstairs?" she says.

You nod. "Upstairs."

You take the first step up the left-hand staircase while Keela takes the right. Dare is still on the main floor, scratching his head in deep thought. "Psst," you whisper to him, "are you coming?"

He looks up absently, as though he doesn't even know where he is. Then he suddenly starts and whips out his broadsword. His head turns quickly from right to left, then he bounds up the right-hand stairs with hardly a breath, crouching defensively at the middle landing. "You must be ready for anything," he says, and he leaps up the stairs and is swallowed by the soundless darkness of the gallery.

"Warriors," you mutter to yourself. "Why couldn't the king have let us thieves off on our own?"

You reach the landing at the same time Keela reaches the opposite landing. You look up into the shadows. The warrior beckons for you with his sword. "Come on! It's safe!" The two of you start up, then come together at the railing of the second floor gallery, which overlooks the great hall.

Twin hallways go off the gallery at the left and right, and you can see at least five or six doors down the right hall. You call your companions over and suggest what to do. "I think we should stay together, like we did in the downstairs rooms. That way, we can't be divided—"

"And conquered," Keela adds.

You nod slowly. The warrior says, "You need have no fear of mortal conflict while I am here. My steel is the strongest in the land, and my brawn—"

"Oh, we know of your might," you interrupt him, smiling. Actually, you are just trying to get him to be quiet. You don't have much time left before the sun goes down, and you've got to get this search over with. If he's given a chance, Dare will probably never shut up about himself. "It's just that we have to expect the unexpected on this quest. And three are mightier than one, don't you agree?"

The fighter nods, unable to fault you for your flawless "warrior" logic.

You start down the right hallway and beckon your companions to follow you. The hallway is lit only by the rays of the setting sun angling through a window at the far end of the hall. Your nose crinkles at the stench of rotted carpet and diseased wood. The carpet is covered in a blanket of gray dust and permeated with black stains from disuse and mildew.

You try the closest door in the hallway and open it. Inside, the bedroom—a woman's room in better days—has been almost destroyed. The canopied bed has been reduced to tatters of soft fabric and chopped pieces of wood, and all the mirrors and pieces of art have been smashed.

The second bedroom is virtually identical in the nature of destruction that has been wreaked across the room. The once beautiful bedspread and mattress have been slashed beyond repair, and the mirrors and the glass in the windows are shattered.

There are ten other bedrooms on the second floor, and in each you find no valuable items or a clue to the whereabouts of the crystal skull. All you find is terrible carnage: the wreckage left from one man's past, destroyed by a dark, violent present that has no room for childhood memories or the love of a family.

After searching the last bedroom upstairs, you close the door and stand in the gallery with your friends. "Back downstairs," the warrior says, and you agree with him. Perhaps it is time for you to search somewhere else. But where?

Go to 25.

20

The warrior grasps the doorknob and twists it until you hear the latch bolt snap back. He takes a deep breath, then heaves open the door with all his strength.

The door bangs against the wall. At once, the warrior leaps in with a loud battle cry. Keela jumps in behind him and spins to the right, and you follow behind her, covering the left side of the room.

The room is long and dark, taking up the entire left side of the first floor, and from its layout you recognize it as the mansion's living room. Ancient paintings hang crookedly on the walls, some slashed, some shot through with arrows. A tapestry hangs in ragged tatters on one wall, and the curtains at the far end of the room sag from their runners, heavy with dust and mildew. Dust lies thick on the stone floor, but there are still places where you can tell where tables, divans, and other furniture had been. Most of it, you're sure, ended up in the bonfire in the great hall.

The three of you split up to search the room. Dare rips the drapes from the wall, and dingy light spills in. You look behind portraits of Fear's long-forgotten family, then tap the walls with the hilt of your sword, listening for the hollow echo that would indicate a secret door. Keela imitates you along the right wall, then stamps her feet across the floor to seek out loose flagstones or hidden entrances.

Throughout the living room, the three of you carry out your search in silence. But the warrior finally speaks up when you meet together at the door.

"There is nothing here," Dare says. "We must search the rest of the mansion."

You sigh in frustration. Through the grimy window, the sun is almost touching the forested hills beyond. There is something here in this mansion, you think. You can almost feel it.

If only you have enough time to find it.

Go to 25.

21

The day has been long and fraught with danger. You feel jittery inside, as though you could not sleep no matter what. Nevertheless, you are drained, exhausted, and you yawn unexpectedly.

Inside the Red Room Inn, you shake Dare's shoulder. The warrior looks up at you sleepily.

"Maybe I can sleep," you tell Dare. "I don't know, but I'll try. Do you mind?"

"No. I'm fine, and the road has been hard. You two try to rest, and I'll wake one of you to take second watch in a few hours."

You unfurl your bedroll and lie down. Your stomach is full; you have just put a few more logs on the fire, so you will all stay warm during the night.

You yawn again and relax upon your bedroll, closing your eyes. You cannot get the image of the walking dead out of your mind, or the chill of the night wind out of your bones. But you sigh deeply, attempting to control the rapid beating of your heart that drums through the unnatural silence that has settled over this village.

Silence . . .

You hear a dim fluttering in the rafters of the Red Room Inn. There, in the shadows above, a gray bird sits atop a rafter. It looks at you calmly, its small eyes reflecting the warmth of the fire, then pecks at something at its feet.

The bird picks up a black ring in its beak. At once, it cries out softly, then takes flight. The ring drops from its beak, and the bird fades away like an old memory.

Your eyes follow the ring as it spins down through the air, slowly, as though it is falling through water. It bounces on the floor soundlessly, then rolls to a stop—

—and a paw reaches out, a massive, heavy paw, with long gray claws and a thick coat of gray fur.

The lion paws the black ring, catching it on a single claw, and drags it in a line across the floor. It looks at you with purpose, its gray eyes gleaming, as though to impart a message. It rears back its shaggy head and shakes out its gray mane, and it roars thunderously, echoing in your ears.

You scream, feeling the terror bubble through your lungs, your throat.

Then you stop yourself, for now you are awake, blinking, gasping, your heart hammering in your chest.

A dream, you think, it was just a dream, a strange, little dream—

Then you look up.

It is much later than you thought. The blaze in the fireplace has died down to embers. The warrior and Keela are sound asleep, undisturbed by your outburst. For a moment, you wonder if they have been bewitched . . . for the inn is alight with the blue glow of witchfire, dancing hypnotically along the tables and walls, the fireplace and bar, in a silent, mesmerizing ballet. You hear its electric song crackling lightly as it plays among the rafters and around the windows.

Then a stronger blue light appears outside the inn's window. It flickers like a ghost on the other side of the glass, and you leap off your bedroll. You shake the others awake and, silently, the three of you watch as the light passes harmlessly through the solid glass and bobs in the air before you. It bounces between the walls and over the tables, then hovers before you, crackling softly, flaring here and there with intensity.

You have never before seen a will-o'-the-wisp, but you have heard the legend, that they are the spirits of the suddenly dead, whose souls burn with needs left unfulfilled in their mortal lives.

The three of you stand cautiously. Dare unsheathes his sword, but you stay his hand. It looks as though the wisp is harmless, perhaps even trying to tell you something.

The witchfire playing through the tavern flickers out, and the ball of blue light slowly bobs away and passes again through the glass window. It hovers outside, passively, glowing with unknown energies.

"I—I think it wants us to follow it," you say.

"That?" Keela says. "Follow that? To where?"

"Cowards," Dare mutters. "Come! Let us find the source of this witchcraft and destroy it!"

"Wait," you say. "It wants us to go with it. I don't sense anything evil about it. Perhaps this has to do with our quest. Perhaps an enemy of Lord Fear has sent this messenger to help us."

Dare considers this. "An enemy of Lord Fear is certainly a friend of ours."

"Right," you say, tightening your sword belt. "Come on. Let's see where this thing goes."

As you open the door to the tavern and step outside, the light dances away, down the street. It travels about a hundred feet, then stops, waiting for you.

You catch up to it, then it dances away again. This goes on for almost ten minutes, and on your walk you think that your eyes are playing tricks on you. You see many strange, impossible sights that you cannot explain, or believe: a black dog, running, its eyes glowing white; a woman's face, weeping, in the leaves of a tree; a dim, scarlet light, wavering in the sky.

Then you are on the far edge of town. Here the houses stop, and you face a long, dark field filled with statues and rectangular objects and monuments that seem frosted with moonlight and shadows.

The witchlight bobs into the village graveyard, weaving between the gravestones and markers as though following a playful maze. In the distance, in the center of the graveyard, the light halts. It hovers above the ground, casting its blue glow on the front of a huge crypt. The letters carved above the iron doors read

ARNSTADT

and as you consider what to do next, the shimmering light passes through the iron gates of the crypt and fades away inside.

You look at each other, then turn again toward the graveyard. Many of the graves appear empty, abandoned . . . from the inside. Lord Fear has been here, you realize, claiming and calling the bodies of the recently dead.

The moon is low, above the horizon. You notice it and point. "Look."

It rises from the earth like a skeletal hand, a black silhouette against the theater of the moon. It is the castle of this lonely realm, Castle Arnstadt, and you know instantly where Lord Fear has taken shelter.

"It wants us to go inside the crypt," you say, turning away from the vision of the black castle. "Lord Fear is nearby, probably holed up in the palace ahead. I think we should find out what this spirit wants."

Keela looks with fear toward the Arnstadt crypt. "I've seen enough dead people today. Why don't we just wait until morning? If Lord Fear is there in the castle, he will be weakest in the daylight. We can grab the crystal skull and run."

Your friend's plan makes sense, and it will probably keep you safe tonight, and you can challenge Fear when he is at his weakest.

But something magical has drawn you out here, and you can sense no evil intent. If Lord Fear has indeed hidden himself in the castle, then you have nothing to be afraid of inside the crypt.

Or do you?

If you wish to enter the crypt, go to 2.

If you decide to return to the inn, go to 46.

22

The undead drop from the drawing room window, giving chase. You cast your gaze toward the front of the mansion, then shout "No!" as a line of shadows march slowly around the corner.

The grounds of Carnivex Mansion are erupting with the undead, placed here by Lord Fear as protection against anyone who might come searching for him. They shamble toward you from inside the mansion, from around the front, and even from the ground before you. One hand pokes out of the earth with torn fingers of bone and clenches spasmodically, grasping emptiness as if breathing the cold night. Then the soil erupts and a head pokes out, dripping with loose soil, and the undead warrior jerks itself slowly from its grave.

Other hands push out from beneath the damp earth, grasping for the living. Soon the countless undead already here will be joined by a score or more of their lifeless brethren, and you will be trapped.

Escape is your only hope, and the only path that lies open to you is to your left, into the forest surrounding Carnivex Mansion—the Forest of Shades. There is a wide break in the trees, as though a large group of warriors passed this way not too long ago. "Follow me!" you shout, turning your steed toward the forest.

Dare and Keela hurriedly spin their horses about and spur them toward you, just as the first few undead get close enough to reach for them with their dead hands of bone. The warrior swings his broadsword in a wide arc, and with the clang of steel cleaving bone, a helmeted skull spins off a skeletal neck and tumbles through the air. The thief's horse, Flame, pounds the skull into the dirt with its mighty hooves, then your companions gallop with you into the forest and toward safety.

You leave the undead chasing after you, their angry eyes burning like scarlet coals. They stop at the edge of the forest, as though by some hidden command, and the

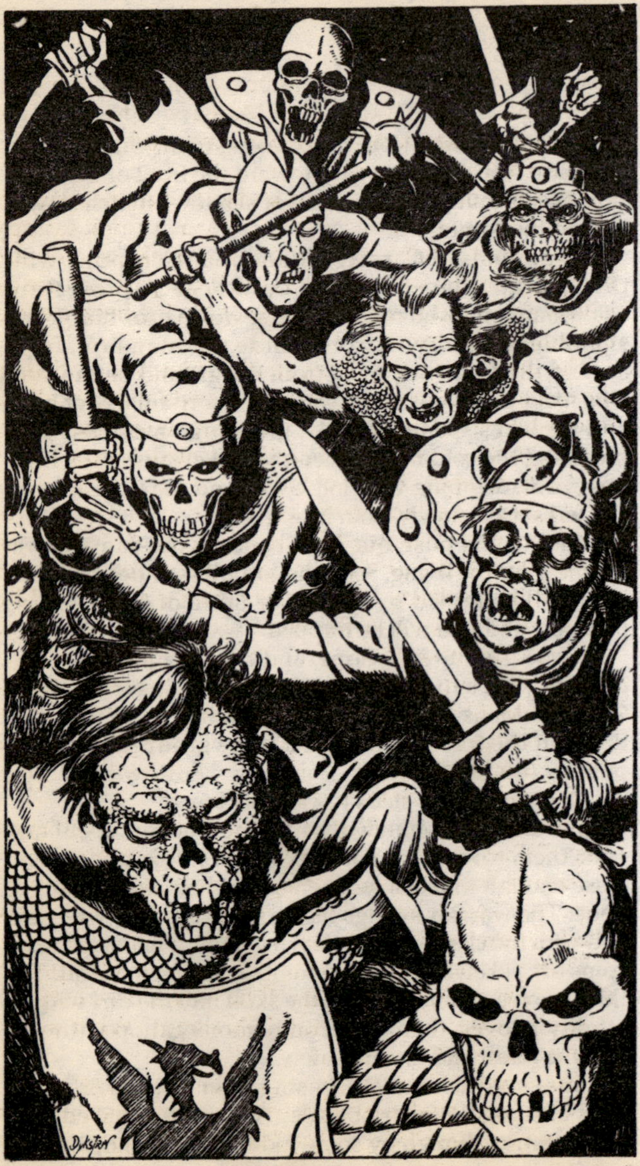

last you see of them is when, as one, they turn and trudge slowly back toward Carnivex Mansion. Then you are swallowed by the darkness of the forest, and you breathe a sigh of relief.

The three of you slow your horses to a more comfortable trot. The overhanging trees form a thick canopy through which very little moonlight peeks, so you are hampered by the lack of light. Luckily, the path you are on is very wide and shows evidence of having been cleared or trampled by an army of men.

The forest is cold and unusually quiet, you notice. In the distance, you hear the hooting of owls and the calls of insects to one another; but the wood seems strange to you, as though it had been invaded. Or haunted. Maybe that is why it is called the Forest of Shades.

You shiver, but not from a chill. "We cannot be sure of our direction in this forest," you say out loud. "We do not know where this path will lead us, but . . ." You hesitate to voice your suspicion. "Since Lord Fear has abandoned his mansion, I wonder if he has taken his army of the undead and gone this way."

Dare rides up beside you, and Keela comes up on the other side. "I think you're right, Shadow," the warrior says. "This must be the road we should take to recover the skull. Fear must be ahead."

"Somewhere," the thief says.

You try to picture the forest and Carnivex Mansion on a map. "What lies ahead in the woods? Do you know?"

Dare shakes his head, but Keela thinks for a few minutes. "A village, I believe, on the other side of the Forest of Shades, near the River Galan."

Then you remember, and a cold chill travels up your spine. "Arnstadt," you tell her. "The village of Arnstadt."

Keela looks at you fearfully. "Arnstadt? What would Fear want there?"

"To conquer," the warrior says. "That much is simple."

"Or to replenish supplies," you continue, your voice almost a whisper. "To build up his legions of the undead."

The thought of Lord Fear conquering an entire village and turning the citizens into undead slaves is more horrifying than you can imagine. You continue on your ride in silence, each of you caught up in your own thoughts and fears. Thankfully, you're confident you have left the undead far behind.

You ride for several hours in the cold darkness, but the path through the forest is relatively level. Soon, moonlight shines through wide gaps in the trees and the going is much easier. Then the Forest of Shades thins out and ends in an uneven line of scraggly trees, and you find yourself on a moonlit plain stretching to the outskirts of the village of Arnstadt.

There are no lights visible in the village, nor is a watchman posted at the village gate. The moon shines down on the sea of grass and the few sparse, twisted trees around you, and you know instinctively that something is terribly wrong in Arnstadt.

The trampled path crosses a road leading directly into the village, and you slow your horse as you approach. On each side of the road—and even *in* the road—strange, gnarled trees are unevenly spaced across the landscape. They stand no higher than six feet tall, and their short branches are leafless, stretching helpless toward the sky. The bark is corded like muscle, twisted, giving an impression of great pain, and when you pass through the silent village gate, you find Arnstadt's streets filled with the trees, hundreds of them, keeping silent vigil in wait for the morning sun.

"Spooky," Keela says.

"I don't like it one bit."

The buildings of the town are abandoned. You all dismount and search quickly through the village square. You find cold, half-eaten meals on tables, and candles burned all the way down. Jewelry and pouches, daggers, swords in their scabbards, and other belongings litter the streets and walkways. The deathly silence here so disturbs you, you don't even want to take anything for fear it be cursed, poisonous to the touch.

A friendly sign hangs above the door of the village tavern, advertising food and drink inside:

The RED RoOM INN

"There," you say. "We can make ourselves a meal and camp there for the night. I don't particularly want to explore much more in the darkness, do you? I think it will be much safer to wait for daylight."

The others are quick to agree, though Dare tries to put on a brave front. You tether your horses outside the inn and unpack your supplies, then cautiously enter the tavern.

The floor is made in a zigzag pattern of light and dark hardwood, and the walls are hidden by long curtains of crimson velvet. Upon everything is a light blanket of dust. A gnarled, miniature version of the strange, lonely trees stands behind the bar, and several of the trees are spaced in a circle around one of the far tables in the tavern.

You drop your supplies on the floor and peer around uneasily. Keela starts a fire in the tavern's fireplace, and soon the Red Room is warm and cozy with the smell of wood smoke, and your bellies are full with foodstuffs you brought from King Halvor's realm. You can almost pretend that everything is normal here.

But not completely. The unease you feel here in Arnstadt refuses to go away. You feel almost as though you are being watched, that you are not alone.

The others unroll their bedding and prepare for the night. "We should alternate watches," Dare says, lying down. "I think we've got at least nine more hours until dawn, so we can all get a few hours of rest. Who wants to keep first watch?"

Although you feel exhausted from the day's events, you just don't know if you will be able to fall asleep here in this deserted village.

If you try to sleep, go to 21.

If you take first watch, go to 37.

23

The air in the great hall turns chill with the advent of night, and with the appearance of the four undead warriors who now approach you, their dead eyes blazing scarlet with the cold fire of undying evil.

The front doors behind you are tightly closed by some evil sorcery, and you cannot get out that way. You rapidly turn your head to examine the other doors leading off the great hall, but the undead are approaching from around the old bonfire in the center, and if you try to escape to the other rooms, you will run right into the skeletal warriors.

The fighter and Keela crowd you, backing in fear against the front doors. Escape, you know, is impossible now. All you can do is take on the undead and hope for the best. You quickly slide your short sword from your belt. Dare looks down at you and smiles. "We'll see what you're made of now, eh, Shadow?"

Then the undead are upon you. Together, the three of you fight like real warriors, driven by honor and desperation to defeat the unholy enemies of the realm.

Sparks fly as your polished steel meets the blade of an undead fighter. Its skeletal mouth opens wide and snaps violently toward you, as though it wants to take the warm, pulsating flesh of your neck between its jaws. Its eyes burn with a sickly fire, and you bring your sword down hard upon its shoulder. Your steel crashes effortlessly through its bones, and its sword arm falls useless to the floor.

Still, the undead trudge mercilessly on. Dare dispatches one fighter with his broadsword and slices the undead warrior into bits of bones. Keela hacks her way across the room, fending off two undead fighters at once. A single strong thrust severs one warrior's head from its neck, and the skeletal body collapses in a heap at her feet. She leaps over it and attacks the other without giving quarter, and in seconds her opponent lies on top of its undead ally. Its helmeted skull chatters for an instant with a deathly grin, then is silent.

You shout for help as your undead opponent closes in on you, weaponless, and takes you into its unholy embrace. Its mouth searches for unprotected flesh, and you can smell its rotting skin and the cold breath of the grave on your neck.

Then the rotting corpse is jerked away from you, and together, the blades of Dare and Keela come down in mighty arcs and slice the undead into pieces of blackened flesh and bones. It falls to the floor, broken and still, its soul having found true death.

You thank your friends, then point your sword toward the door. "We obviously can't get out that way. We've got to do something before—"

You speak too late, for the floor in the great hall buckles in spots, as though something with great strength is pushing up from the earth below. Then tile and wood and brick explode upward, and a score of undead warriors shamble out of their graves underneath the floor and face you, their rusted and tarnished weapons at the ready, and they stare at you with their fiery, evil eyes.

You cannot hope to fight them and win; even Dare can see you have no chance. Your only recourse is to—

"Run!" you scream, and the three of you tear across the room. The warrior starts toward the door to the right, but you shout, "No! The window in the drawing room! It's our only hope!"

Dare turns faster than you ever would have thought possible and crashes through the drawing room door. The window in front of you is broken, and through it you see the forest beyond.

Dare leaps. The heavy drape hanging beside the window catches in the fighter's hand, and he whips it before him for protection as his body hurtles through panes of sharp glass and thick splinters of wood. He falls to the ground outside as glass rains around him; then he is up and running toward the front of the mansion.

You jump to the window ledge. Keela comes up beside you. Quickly, you look behind you, and the undead warriors are filing through the doorway, following you hungrily.

You and Keela look each other in the eyes, then jump.

You come down hard, but like any agile thief, you roll with the impact to lessen the fall. Then you leap to your feet. The thief is already up, and Dare is galloping around the corner upon Arrow, the other horses in tow. You leap into Bentley's saddle as the first few undead drop from the window to give chase.

The road away from the mansion stretches into the distance, but to your right you see an uneven gap in the trees, as though something big had made its way through the woods not so long ago.

The undead are almost upon you. You must decide what to do immediately.

Desperately, you shout, "This way!"

If you take the road that brought you to Carnivex Mansion, go to 7.

If you enter the woods, go to 22.

24

You think about the pile of debris up here in the attic, then compare your chances to finding something downstairs in the conservatory. The trash in the room seems like nothing more than useless junk, and the conservatory is huge. Sure, it is very dark in there, and you don't like the feeling of fear that comes over you when you think about the greenhouse. But you haven't searched there yet, and almost anything could be hidden in there. . . .

You make up your mind, though you don't particularly like your decision.

"I think we should go back downstairs," you tell your companions. "Let's search the conservatory."

They nod in agreement, and the three of you make your way down the secret stairs. At the bottom, you leave through the fireplace and close the secret door. You stand before the conservatory entrance, contemplating your actions.

Go to 67.

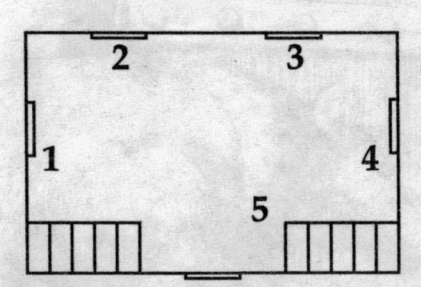

25

You enter the great hall again and stop beside the pile of charred debris in the center of the great hall. There are four other places you can search. You can also retrace your previous steps—but why bother? You searched it thoroughly, and there is nothing there for you to find.

Finally, you make up your mind. "That one," you say.

If you enter door 1, go to 20.

If you enter door 2, go to 10.

If you enter door 3, go to 49.

If you enter door 4, go to 43.

If you go up the stairs, go to 19.

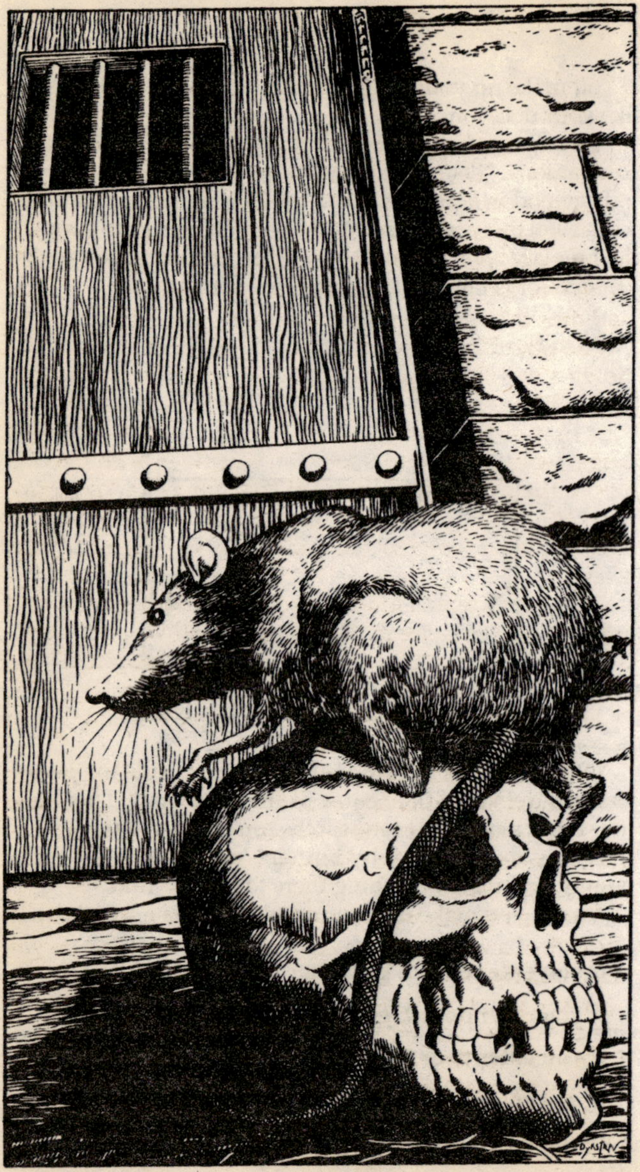

26

"Shadow, the thief of the Emerald Collar of the Lady Carnassia—among other things!" the guard shouts at the thick, iron-bolted door.

An iron plate slides open in the door, and a guard inside peers out at you, the newest prisoner to the king's dungeon. You hear keys being turned in four heavy locks, and then the door slowly creaks open.

The guard behind you pushes you on, and you start down a winding, stone staircase, lit very dimly by a few weak torches placed on the walls. You have never been in this part of the dungeon before; you've seen only the huge, central chamber where you were kept with the others on the night of the ball. This portion is darker, grimmer. The walls and steps are coated with a thick growth of moss, and you can feel the dank moistness against your skin.

The guard opens another heavy wooden portal and pushes you into a long, dim corridor with doors on each side. From behind the doors come cries of "Help me!" and "I didn't do anything!"

"Everybody's innocent in the king's dungeon," your guard says, laughing.

From behind the doors, you hear sad weeping, sometimes moaning. Someone pounds on the inside of a door. "Let me out of here!" the prisoner yells. Laughter comes from another cell, the mad, gibbering laughter of the hopelessly insane.

The guard jerks you to a stop. He turns a large key in the lock of a wooden door, then his heavy foot shoves you deep into the cell.

A key twists in the lock of your shackles, then your hands are free, and the guard stands alone in the doorway, framed by flickering torchlight. The guard indicates the thin layer of dry straw on the floor.

"Make yourself comfortable, Shadow. You're going to be here a long time. But don't worry—we won't forget you, like some of the others."

The prisoner who had laughed suddenly breaks out into a rambling drinking song, and raises a high note into a piercing, insane scream. The guard smiles. "The king will get to you eventually, thief. You'll be tried, and then you'll hang from the gallows for your crimes." He shrugs. "But enjoy your stay. It could be worse," he says. "At least you have company."

The door slams shut and locks. Behind it, the guard's laugh fades as he walks away.

You scream in terror as you spy your cellmates.

The rat is fat and ugly, watching you as it sits atop the gnawed skull of a skeleton shackled to the wall, a long-forgotten prisoner in the king's chamber of horrors. As the guard's footsteps disappear into the distance, you realize that the dead and the insane are your only friends down here in the dungeon of the forgotten, and that this prisoner's fate will turn out to be your own.

You hide your head in your arms and curl up for warmth. Beside you, the rat chitters hungrily, watching you with its red, beady eyes. You cannot take it any longer, and you scream once, long and violently, and pound the stone floor with your hands. You cry out, "Just give me one more chance!" But no one hears you, save for your fellow inmates, and it slowly dawns on you that you will probably never see the light of day again in your lifetime.

You look at the black rat. It is sitting up, watching you with its piercing eyes. "Halvor," you say, realizing that at least you've got someone else to talk to. You reach out a hand to pet the vermin. "I think I'll name you Halvor, king of the rats."

And you laugh. You laugh and laugh, until your throat is raw, and the echoes ring loudly in your ears.

The End

27

You look at the pile of chairs and wood in the center of the floor and say, "No, I think there might be something up here." You start in on the pile, lifting off a ratty, old chair, then several books written in a tongue unknown to you. Keela sighs and approaches to help you. Dare comes closer, holding up the torch for you to see.

You look up at him. "You better stay back," you say. "If even a spark flies off that torch, this pile could go up faster than kindling."

Dare stops suddenly, then takes a few steps back. "Ohh."

When she reaches into the middle of the pile, Keela uncovers a portrait of a family. This painting has not been subjected to the damage that the paintings downstairs have, and you can make out a mother and father, and a thin, sallow-faced boy standing between them. His eyes seem black and hollow, soulless, and you shudder with a sudden chill.

"Lord Fear," Keela tells you. "He did not change much when he grew up. Even as a child, he must have been an acolyte of the black arts."

You look at Lord Fear's parents. Their eyes are almost as dark as Fear's, and the symbol on Lord Carnivex's tunic is that of a black, bat-winged dragon—the symbol of a secret society of blood drinkers. "Perhaps the black arts are a Carnivex family tradition," you say. You take the painting and throw it aside. "Let's hurry up and get out of here. The farther away from the Carnivex estate, the better."

In the pile you find a volume of journal entries written by a Carnivex scholar over two centuries ago, and under that a wooden box filled with old tools and iron nails. You toss everything aside and continue through the pile, until finally your hand closes around a smooth length of wood on the bottom of the pile. You pull it out from under an old chair and turn it in your hands, watching the golden torchlight sparkle off its bands of gold and its crest of silver.

You have found an ornate, decorative walking stick, carved from a single piece of rare ernith, a redwood found only in the farthest reaches of the northern wastes. At its tip and in bands encircling the wood, the torchlight glimmers off rings of gold, and the top of the walking stick is dominated by a four-fingered fist crafted in shining silver. The fingers are long and tapered, like claws, terminating with razor-sharp tips, and each unhuman finger has three knuckles.

Your eyes widen in surprise as you turn the stick around in your hands. This is it, you realize. This is what you have been looking for throughout Carnivex Mansion. You don't know anything about a crystal skull; instinctively, you know that this is what your search here as been all about.

The others stand around you while you examine your find. "Do you have any idea what that is?" the thief asks you. You shake your head, and the warrior speaks up. "Can't you thieves do anything right? We're here to find the crystal skull, not a piece of old garbage."

You nod at him innocently. This thing has gold on it, and this fighter calls it garbage? "Of course, of course. And find the skull we shall. I cannot help it if we have found this meager prize as well."

"The skull is obviously not here," Keela says. "Lord Fear has escaped with it, and who knows where he might be now?"

Dare shrugs. "What do I care if you don't find the skull? They are your lives, not mine. I'm just following my liege's orders to safeguard you on your quest. Nothing more."

Your quest. The joy of finding the ornate walking stick had caused you to momentarily forget that this quest is your only chance for freedom. Absently, you look for a way to carry the walking stick safely. You won't need to use it while on horseback. You look down at your new, velvet pouch. It is far too small for anything the size of a walking stick, but it would fit nicely over the silver crest and protect it on your ride.

You tug open the golden drawstring and slip the pouch over the top of the stick. You blink for a second, your whole body tingling with a surge of warm energy, and the pouch easily engulfs the head of the staff, and then swallows the walking stick's entire length.

"What wizardry is this?" you cry out. You open the mouth of the pouch wide enough to peer inside. The others crowd around you, Dare holding the torch close enough to cast light into the bag.

The staff is tucked safely inside the small pouch, impossibly held in a sea of blackness, as though an entire universe could be found inside the folds of your pouch. You remember the elven words stitched into the side of the bag—*infinity*—and you realize that the pouch you have found is truly a magical item, the stuff of legends. You have heard tales and supposed myths of bottomless pouches said to open onto an endless storeroom or, perhaps, another boundless universe. And now you've found one, where all your belongings can be safely stored or carried, and where enemies will never find your most precious treasures.

Dare swallows nervously, both amazed and horrified at the magic he has witnessed. Warriors do not much like sorcery, for they generally dislike anything intellectual or creative. He looks at you strangely. "You are not a wizard," he says, as though he is just realizing that. "Where did you come by such a thing as that pouch?"

"I have had it for years," you say without thinking, for how can you admit to this loyal servant of the king that you stole it from the king's vault? "It has been handed down in my family for decades."

Dare looks at you with distrust. But he has no time to react, for Keela beside you suddenly grabs your arm, an urgent look across her lovely features. "How can we be so stupid?" she says. "What are we doing talking up here? It is sundown! We have to get out!"

You look about wildly for a window, but there is none up in this secret attic chamber. You give Dare no time to further question you about the pouch. "Come on! We've got to go now!"

You rip the torch out of Dare's hand and plunge into the stairwell. You practically leap down the curving stairs, the pouch bouncing lightly against your hip as though it were empty. The others follow behind you so closely you can almost feel their breaths on your neck.

Six steps away from the bottom, you jump off the stairs and roll agilely toward the secret door in the fireplace. You jump into the drawing room and turn toward the glass wall of the conservatory. You hear the others come up behind you, and you softly say, staring through the glass, "The sun has already gone down."

The three of you say nothing. Then, as though on some private, unspoken signal, you all bolt for the great hall. You speed around the bonfire in the center of the hall and turn toward the front doors . . .

. . . which are now closed. You rush over to the doors and twist the handles in both hands, but somehow they have been locked; the handles will not budge, and the doors will not open even an inch, as though they are being held tight by some magical bonds.

"I can't open them," you stammer. "Something is holding them together. Look!" You point to the latch, in the crack between the thick doors. "The lock isn't on! Someone has blocked us in here with a spell!"

Behind you, you hear the whisper of the trees, a rattle, as though of bones jangling in the earth. The three of you turn around slowly.

They come from around the pile of charred debris, dragging their white, fleshless bones against the gray stone floor. There are four of them, warriors of the undead, staring at you with their dead eyes of scarlet fire, grinning at you with bone-white smiles and laughter like hisses from the grave.

Their armor is rusted and ancient, the leather joints rotting and dangling from their elbows and knees in blackened tatters. Their shields are pitted with disuse, still stained with the earth from their graves, and their swords, no matter how dull, can still be wielded with an unnatural, deadly strength.

A whiff of decomposition, of rot, comes to your nose, and the voices of the undead echo softly around you, reverberating in an obscene litany. As one, they speak in a chilling mockery of the voice of their terrible master.

Cursed be you who trespass here! You who come to plunder, the house of Carnivex shall become your tomb! There will be no escape! Beware the wrath of Fear! Prepare to serve a new master for all eternity!

The undead warriors shamble toward you. Their swords gleam wickedly in the dim torchlight, and the three of you unsheathe your blades and prepare to meet the attack of the undead.

Quickly, you look around. The stairs leading to the second floor are useless; there is no escape up there. But you still have time to try to escape through the other rooms downstairs.

The undead number only four, and with Dare on your side, they might prove quite easy to defeat. You can move faster than they can, and you have something they don't: the ability to think independently.

If you decide to fight, go to 23.

If you decide to escape, go to 45.

28

The landscape at Castle Arnstadt is bleak and gray. The air is still and unnaturally cool, and you spur your horses across the empty courtyard to the entrance of the castle's fortresslike keep.

The keep is a tall, cylindrical tower built out of ancient stone. Dare tests the doors for traps or spells, but there are none. The doors are unlocked, as you knew they would be, for Lord Fear's arrogance does not let him believe that he has any reason to worry about a threat from mere mortals.

The tall wooden doors at the entrance open into a gloomy foyer whose inner doors are closed. Twin stairways on each side of the foyer lead up to the second level, which is unlit. A small doorway is open under the left-hand stairway.

The inner doors are unlocked and unprotected by magic.

"Three ways," the warrior says. "How do you want to do this?"

If you go upstairs, go to 59.

If you go through the inner doors, go to 51.

If you go through the small doorway, go to 47.

29

The evidence in the royal vault was slight. Yes, it seems as though Lord Fear and his undead servants were the ones who stole the crystal skull, but you do not know that for sure. Perhaps a visit to this wizard in the wilderness can help you find the skull a little bit sooner.

"The footprints in the vault may have been left there deliberately, to throw us off the true thief's track," you tell them. "A wizard might be perfect. He might be able to tell us exactly where the skull is and how to get it."

Dare scowls. "Sorcery!" he spits.

The three of you start off down the forest path. In an hour, you come to a narrow, little-used path forking off from the main road. This is the old mountain road, which is seldom used since Calina, the city in the mountains, was mysteriously abandoned by its inhabitants many years ago, and the population disappeared.

The road is overgrown with grass and is pitted from disuse. The going is slow on horseback, but by dusk you are well inside the mountainous region. The golden spires and ruins of Calina shine in the light of the setting sun. Your eyes are pulled toward the sight of the ruined metropolis carved into the mountain, and you can imagine Calina when it was alive and populated, a city of wonders and brilliance.

But Keela pulls your attention away and points to a dark area at the base of the mountain. You spur Bentley on and pull up at the mouth of a cave, artfully hidden by scrub brush and trees.

The three of you dismount. Keela steps behind the trees and cups her hands around her mouth, and she signals down into the cave using the sound of an owl. Three times

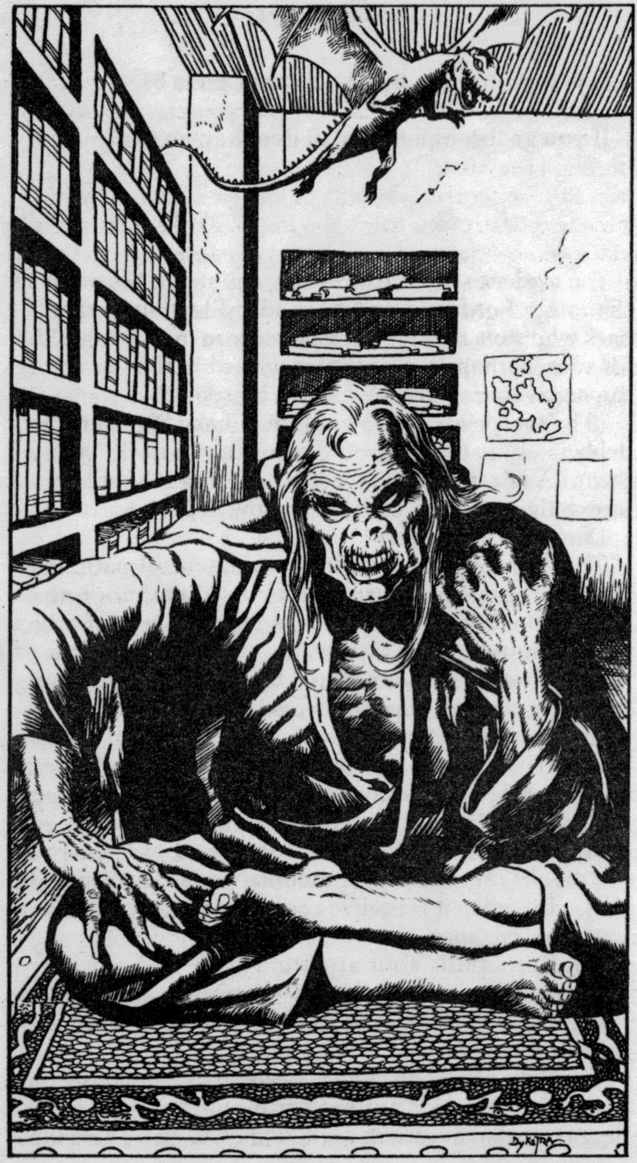

she calls with the voice of an owl, then she beckons for you and Dare to follow her. "It is a signal," she says. "With that, Lo'tak cancels the magical traps he has placed all through the cave."

You step under the overhang of the trees and find yourself in the mouth of the cave. You follow Keela until it gets so dark you cannot see, then the cave makes a sharp turn and you are in a stone antechamber, lit by torches on the walls, and a flight of carved stairs leads down into blackness. Keela takes a torch out of the sconce in the wall and leads you down the stone stairs.

The stone steps have no railing, and you find yourself hugging the rough, cool wall as you descend. The temperature grows cooler the farther you proceed under the earth. You can smell the dankness here where the sun never shines, and soon the steps are slick with moss and black fungi.

At the base of the stairs, you come to a single wooden door. Dare steps forward and knocks loudly on the ancient wood. "Mage," he shouts, "we come from the king! We must speak with you!"

The handle starts to turn, then the door swings open slowly. Dare takes a step and stops. The door is opening by itself.

"Come in," a calm voice says from deep inside the room. The room has been carved into the rock, and from the doorway you can see walls of ancient books and shelves laden with hundreds of scrolls and parchments. From the ceiling hangs the embalmed corpse of a winged lizard, and on the unshelved walls hang maps and diagrams, alongside painted sketches of arcane designs and patterns.

The mage rises from a cross-legged position in the rear of the room. The ornamental carpet beneath him folds itself neatly.

"Ahh, thief," he says, greeting Keela and kissing her on the back of her hand. "Welcome, welcome. It has been too long." He turns to you. "I am Lo'Tak," he says, bowing slightly. He is a tall man dressed in swirling robes of purple and black. His skin is stretched tightly across his face, giving him a mummified appearance, but his voice is even and strong, and you have no idea how old this wizard is.

You return the bow. "I am Shadow," you say, "and we come to you on a mission of urgency. My friend says you may be able to help us."

The wizard's eyes seem to glow. "Ahh, yes. Shadow. So you are the reckless thief I have seen so much about in my crystals." The wizard smiles thinly, and you dimly think that it is the coldest smile you have ever seen. "Please come in and be seated. I believe we have much to discuss."

You introduce Dare, and the wizard seats you among a pile of soft, richly padded furs and cushions. The room smells of exotic incense and aromas from around the world, from places you can only dream of visiting. Maybe when this quest is over, you will have enough time and enough gold to adventure across the globe.

In a corner, the mage begins to boil a pot of tea for your party. He places a pot of water and tea leaves on a metal stand. He utters a single word, and a blue flame erupts underneath the pot, licking the base with violet tongues. "Now how may I be of service to you, my friends?" the wizard asks.

"We seek the Crystal Skull of Sa'arkloth," you tell him bluntly. "It has been stolen from the treasury of King Halvor, and we have been entrusted with its safe return."

The wizard faces you, his mouth agape. "The crystal skull? But it was supposed to have perished in the magma pool from whence it had come."

"That was the legend," Keela says. "The truth is that the skull was kept by the king's mage, Taurokkus, and given to the king for safekeeping. Taurokkus knew that the skull's powers were too great a temptation even for him."

"Now the skull has been stolen," you say, "and the evidence points toward Lord Fear as the thief."

DUNGEON OF FEAR 75

Lo'Tak turns away and busies himself with the tea. "Lord Fear . . ." he says to himself. He opens the teapot and sprinkles chopped green leaves into the water, then pours the tea into three cups.

The mage brings over the cups and passes them around, then sits beside you upon his cushions. The tea is hot and pleasant after your long ride; sweet at first, then becoming slightly bitter on the aftertaste, and you absently wonder what the green leaves were that the wizard dropped into the tea.

"So, the crystal skull has resurfaced at last," Lo'Tak says. "Taurokkus, you know, was a fool. Together, we could have used the skull to conquer the realm. But Taurokkus was too kind. He had no ambition whatsoever."

You blink as though dazed. Lo'Tak knew Taurokkus? But how? It must have been so long ago . . .

You look around. Keela seems to have problems keeping her eyes open, and Dare is blinking, shaking his head, as though he is trying to ward off sleep. Then you dimly realize that you feel sluggish, as though your movements are slow. Lo'Tak is smiling at each one of you in turn, and you remember that the mage is the only one who did not drink any tea.

The wizard stands. You try to move, but you are paralyzed. Whatever he put in the tea, it has sapped your strength. You are not sleepy at all, but you have been drained of the strength and the will to move.

"It was I who did battle with Taurokkus at the Valley of Stars, for I am KorLu, returned to wreak revenge upon my enemies. In the Valley of Stars, Taurokkus defeated me with a powerful spell, and I thought he destroyed the skull by throwing it into the pit where it was discovered a thousand years ago. But that, too, must have been a spell of illusion. Instead, he let the world think the skull was gone forever, and he kept it for himself. Amazing! His cunning then exceeded even my own."

Lo'Tak smiles and looks into your eyes. "Poor, foolish thieves. You did not know what you were doing by coming to me. Do not worry about retrieving the skull, for that obligation—that pleasure—shall be all mine." The wizard laughs uproariously, and his laughter echoes throughout the cave. "The skull shall be mine once again! And with its power, I will finally bring the powers of darkness to the realm, and claim the throne as my own!"

He turns sharply away, and his robes swirl out as he strides toward a series of tall shelves filled with vials and bottles and jars of liquids and potions and powders and ingredients. He opens a jar filled with a pink powder and takes a pinch between his fingers. He stands above the three of you and looks down with mock compassion. "I cannot kill you, no—for you were kind enough to bring me the knowledge that the skull still survives. But I cannot have you going off to warn the king, now can I, hmm? I think not."

With a flourish, the mage lets the powder fall upon the three of you. It tingles on your skin, then you feel its warmth growing throughout your body. The wizard touches you with one bony finger. "Ground sniffer," he says. He touches Dare and says, "Pond hopper," then touches Keela and says to her, "Tree climber."

Your stomach clenches into a tight ball, and the world around you spins. Everything is clouded in a swirling pink haze, and when you open your eyes, you vaguely think that the cave is much larger, and that the wizard has grown an incredible height.

He reaches down and plucks you from the floor, then does the same with the frog and the squirrel that are moving slowly around his feet.

You would be scared if you could be, but you can no longer think very well, the way you once did. The wizard holds you up before a mirror, and your last human thoughts are how pretty the dark rings around your eyes are, and how bushy your tail is.

Several minutes later, you find yourself on the ground outside the cave. Your companions, the frog and the squirrel, hop away toward the forest, and you follow them slowly, sniffing the ground for traces of food.

The concerns of life in the realm are now unimportant. The wizard will have his skull and will conquer the king's armies with the powers of darkness, but you will be safe in the wood, where streams will satisfy your thirst and insects will be your meals. Your life as a thief is now over, and your existence as a raccoon in the forest has begun.

The End

30

Perhaps escape is possible, you think. But that's the home of Lord Fear up ahead, and Keela should not have to go in that place alone with the king's warrior. You got into this to help her out, didn't you? You can't help her any if you try to back out now. She needs someone with cunning and skill, not a pea-brained lunkhead who can lift a ton but can't spell it.

You snap the reins of your steed, and Bentley moves on through the broken gate. On the ground is a dirty oval sign made out of brass. Across the surface, tarnished with age and black mildew, engraved letters read

Carnivex Estate

You sigh. What's that quote? In for a copper, in for a gold?

How do you get yourself into these things?

The dirt path leading from the gate is overgrown with grass, and you're very careful not to let your horse stumble in one of the stagnant puddles of water spotting the path. From the disuse, it is very obvious that no one has been to this place in a long time. Nonetheless, you keep watch on all sides and strain your ears for any unusual sounds . . . for who knows what lies in wait for unwary visitors at the home of Lord Fear?

You notice something odd: the air is deathly still, and even with the afternoon sunlight, the air here is cooler, and the light seems darker, or muted. Perhaps you have less time before sundown than you thought.

Dare's horse, Arrow, suddenly stops, unwilling to go any farther. It snorts in frustration, but Dare pushes the steed on, and your group rounds a bend in the path and comes upon the front of Carnivex Mansion.

Unconsciously, all of you stop short upon your first clear view of the mansion. The house is huge and dark: two stories of gray stone and wood, a dark, gabled roof protecting an attic, and walls and windows covered with blackened creepers of ivy. Its windows are mostly broken or shattered, and moldy curtains hang lifeless in the absence of a breeze. It stretches across your view like a large, squat bug, coldly watching its innocent prey.

The house is dead, and you most definitely do not want to go in there. You shudder once, involuntarily, and notice the others looking up at the house with the same expression of awe and dread that you have. Dare is the first to recover, shaking himself deliberately, then forcing a smile. "Well, come on!" he yells. "It looks like nobody has been home for a long time! What do we have to worry about? There's no Lord Fear here!"

You're not so sure about that. Despite the appearance of emptiness, this could be an elaborate trap that Lord Fear has set for anyone on his trail. Your hand goes to the hilt of the short sword at your waist. You're not a skilled warrior, but when you've been in trouble before, you've always fought—or thought—your way out.

You carefully dismount Bentley and tether him to an iron railing. A long staircase of stone leads up to the shattered wooden doors that had been the main entrance. The others dismount, then together the three of you start up the stairs. Your steps are sure and careful, and you notice the others making sure that their weapons are ready for any eventuality. The warrior carries a broadsword, a short sword, and a shield emblazoned with the crest of King Halvor. Thieves like you are different from most fighters: you care more for lightness and speed, and so you carry only a short sword and a dagger, as does Keela, who is without her customary bullwhip.

The wooden doors are tall, at least ten feet high, and more than five inches thick. The doors had been fixed with heavy iron hinges, yet something had ripped through them with unimaginable power, splintering them into shards of pale wood and bending the ironwork like butter. "Could the skull have done all this?" you say to yourself.

But in the strange silence, the others hear you. Keela says, "I hope not. This is worse than I could have dreamed."

"Sorcery!" Dare says, spitting into the darkened entrance. "Wizards are nothing without their accursed spells. Give me a man to fight, armed with only sharpened steel, any day."

The warrior steps past the broken doors and into the darkness inside. Keela trails him, and, with a nervous swallow, you follow her close behind.

You are inside a large foyer that had once been paneled in beautiful wood. Now everything has been ruined by the elements and by deliberate destruction. Weak sunlight filters through windows and the open doors, casting gray light upon the shards of wood and debris littering the foyer floor. Mold and mildew have crept up the walls in velvety black splotches, and your nose is filled with the pungent tang of rot settling into the walls and floors.

There are two doors in front of you, one hanging loose from its hinges. Beyond you can see only a glimmer of light shining off a grimy marble floor. You take your short sword from its scabbard and point into the house. "I guess we should go in," you say, a tremble in your voice.

No one says anything. The warrior turns, and for an instant you see a reflection of fear on his sculpted features. Then his eyes seem to grow dark with determination, and he wheels upon the door, kicking out with one booted foot. The right-hand door suddenly bursts off its remaining hinge and spins into the room beyond. Dare screams with a berserker yell and dives through the open doorway, his long sword brandished in front of him. You and the thief exchange astonished glances. Perhaps there is use for a knuckle-headed warrior after all.

You find yourself inside a rectangular hall. Immediately to the left and right are long stairs leading up to the second floor gallery, and from there into the darkness above. The center of the great hall is filled with a tall pile of the blackened, charred remains of furniture and tapestries, of ancient books and various items that could easily burn. Scorch marks from the blaze have blackened the ceiling high above and parts of the surrounding walls.

Aside from the doors leading to the foyer and back outside, there are four other doors in the hall, all closed: two on the long wall in front of you, and doors on each wall to the left and right.

You circle the remains of the bonfire and are amazed that the blaze did not destroy the mansion. It must have simply died out prematurely; and all the better for you, for a deliberate fire of this size was most certainly set to destroy the house. At least now you have a chance to explore the background of Lord Fear, and to find the crystal skull.

The female thief speaks up, and her words echo strangely in the abandoned house. "I don't think anyone is home," she says.

"We must search the villain out wherever he may be," Dare says. "We have much to do in very little time."

"Someone set this fire deliberately," you say, "to keep people out of the house."

"Lord Fear has fled," Dare says. "He burned his home so no one could follow him."

DUNGEON OF FEAR 81

"Aye," the thief answers. "This mansion has been in ruins for a long while. Perhaps when Nevill Carnivex took the title of Lord Fear—and became almost a new person with a new identity—he destroyed his ancestral home as well."

"He burned his past in favor of a new identity," you say. "Nevertheless, we still need the skull. Just in case, we must search this place, and quickly.

"But we must be very careful," you add. "Anything could be waiting for us behind these doors. Anything."

You look behind you through the open doors leading outside. The sun will soon set, and you have to decide where to search.

You raise your sword and point. "Let's go in here!"

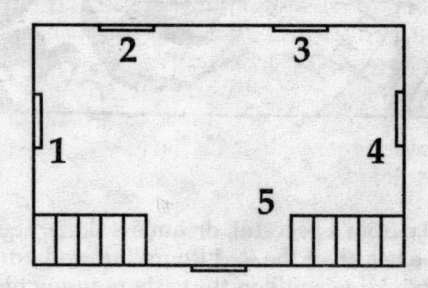

If you enter door 1, go to 20.

If you enter door 2, go to 10.

If you enter door 3, go to 49.

If you enter door 4, go to 43.

If you want to search upstairs, go to 19.

31

You wake from a peaceful, dreamless sleep. The fire has died on the hearth of the Red Room Inn, and outside the stars are twinkling softly in the early morning night. You lie there quietly, at rest for the first time in what seems like years, listening to the birds chirping outside.

Birds! You get up and step outside the door. The air is calm and fresh, and you hear birds singing in the nearby forest.

Lord Fear is gone, you think. His evil has been destroyed, and the birds and animals are coming back home.

You take a deep breath of the morning air and sigh contentedly. You never imagined that you would be the one to dispatch Lord Fear and retrieve the skull from his evil grasp, but you did it. You quite possibly saved not only King Halvor's realm from his tyranny, but the entire world.

DUNGEON OF FEAR

You smile to yourself. Shadow, you did it.

Inside, the others are waking in the hour before dawn, anxious to leave Arnstadt and return home. The three of you pack your supplies and eat a warm breakfast, then you step outside to where your horses wait.

The sky is lightening softly in the east, and as you turn toward the horizon, you see the first timid shafts of sunlight poke through a mass of clouds on the horizon, and through the bare branches of the strange trees scattered through the village.

Dawn, you think. Sunlight. So much better than the promise of Lord Fear's eternal darkness.

You reach up to straddle Bentley, your horse, then stop. Dawn. There's something you should remember about the dawn. . . .

If you took the rubies from Lord Fear's vault and have them in your pouch, go to 13.

If not, go to 66.

32

"Hold on!" you shout, jumping to your feet. "She has done nothing wrong! She's been here in the tavern with me!"

The captain of the guard grows red in the face, and his features contort grotesquely, making him appear uglier than humanly possible. "And just who are you to defend a known thief of the realm?" he asks, growling. "Or are you a criminal, too?" The other guards pull their long swords from their scabbards.

"Me?" you say innocently. "No, I'm nobody."

The captain stares at you. "Then nobody shouldn't be butting his head in somebody else's business." He hands Keela to the other guards, who take a pair of heavy iron shackles and clamp them around her wrists.

"Understand?"

You understand all too well the trouble Keela is in. And you'll be in the same trouble if you try to help her. But what else can you do? She's Keela.

"Well, what is she accused of then? You can at least tell us that."

The rest of the tavern has grown silent as all the patrons watch the altercation, expectantly waiting for a fight of some kind. The captain of the guard looks around and grunts with exasperation. The crowd is made up more of your friends than his, and he knows it.

"I have my orders, peasant," he says. He places his thick hand against your chest and shoves you back down into your chair effortlessly. "Now, don't you cause any trouble, or we'll take the two of you in just as easily as one."

You place your hands on the table and stand up again. You look the captain right in his piglike eyes. "I don't want any trouble, guardsman," you say, "I just want to know what my friend has done. She has been in here, sitting with me."

From a far corner, someone yells, "Tell us!"

Someone else in the room shouts, "What did she do?"

The captain keeps his eyes on you. His face gets redder, his eyes narrower. He knows that Keela is well-liked in the Rose and Crown, and this could cause a problem. He can't arrest everybody in the tavern, but you can see that the guard is laying the blame for all this trouble on you.

The captain says it loud enough for all to hear, but he never takes his eyes off you. "This thief is being taken for an audience with the king. She is accused of robbery!"

The guard's proclamation has the opposite effect of what he intended. The people in the tavern start to laugh, including you and Keela. "Robbery?" Keela says, laughing proudly. "What do you expect me to do? I'm a thief."

The guard takes a step toward her. "Is this an admission that you are guilty?"

She laughs in his face. "No! But tell me, who am I supposed to have robbed?"

The laughter dies down, and the guard says, "You are accused of robbing the king himself, by breaking into the royal treasury and murdering three innocent guards."

Silence falls over the tavern. "The royal . . ." Keela starts to say, but her voice trails off in astonishment. To rob the treasury right under the nose of the king himself would be unheard of. You know from firsthand experience, of course, for you once toyed with the idea of breaking into the king's vault yourself. But it was too well guarded, and you—just like Keela—cannot kill anyone in cold blood.

You instantly know Keela was not the burglar who broke into the treasury, for she would never kill wantonly, nor would she kill the guards, or anyone else who was just doing their jobs.

"She's not the one you're looking for," you say.

The guards start toward the door, dragging the struggling Keela between them. The captain of the guard looks you over. His dull eyes focus on your face, and they seem to spark with an inner light, as if he recognizes you from somewhere. "And just how would you know? Or are you saying it was you who robbed the treasury?"

"No, of course I didn't rob the vault. But neither did she. She may be of the thieves' guild, but she has never been a murderer."

The captain steps closer, and you can smell his hot breath on your face. "I know you . . ." he says.

You swallow nervously. "I—I don't think so, Captain," you say. "I wish you'd listen to me. She is innocent. Of that I'm—"

"You!" he says, and his huge hand leaps out and grabs you roughly by the shoulder. "You! You are the one called Shadow!"

You shake your head madly. "No, no, I'm just a simple traveler—"

"Hah!" the guard cries. His companions stop at the

door. Keela looks back and realizes the predicament you're in.

"The king probably will give me a promotion for bringing you in, thief," the captain says. "Why, I'd wager that the two of you broke into the treasury together, and you were surprised by the guards. I wouldn't put even murder past the notorious Shadow."

"Hey, wait a minute!" you shout. "I didn't break into the vault, and I didn't murder anybody!"

Keela kicks one of the guards in the gut, then drives her shoulder into the other guard's chin. "Run, Shadow!" Get out of here!"

The guards struggle to recover. The captain slides out his sword and bares his teeth in a grim smile. "Come on, Shadow," he says. "Take me on. I dare you."

All you've got on you is a dagger. You reach for it involuntarily, but there is no use: you're practically helpless against this mammoth of a man. At the door, Keela has been secured by the guards, and she watches you with fear in her eyes, as though she is thinking, Go, Shadow! Get out of here while you can!

This is not the time, and you realize it. If you try to fight your way out, you'll never see the sunshine again, and the prisoners in the king's dungeon will be your only friends. But if you go peacefully, there's always a chance you can sneak your way out of this trouble sooner or later.

You take your hand off the dagger and hold your wrists out. "Take me in, Captain," you say, a sly smile across your face. "Yes, I'm Shadow. And I'm your prisoner. But I'm not a murderer, and neither is my friend. Take us in if you wish, but I vow that we shall prove our innocence, and we will go free."

The guard takes a set of manacles off his belt and snaps them around your wrists. "Free, eh? We'll see about that."

The guards lead you through the tavern while the patrons silently watch. When you reach the door, Nash calls out from behind the bar, "There is honor among thieves! Come back when you can, Shadow. Your meal and drinks are on me!"

The tavern breaks out in cheers, then you are shoved outside, into the daylight. The people in the market stop their business and stare as you are jostled toward the keep. You hear cries throughout the bazaar of "They got him!" and "They've taken Shadow!" A woman shouts, "Don't tell them where the collar is! The Carnassias are tyrants!" One merchant you know steps away from his stall and yells out, "Stand tall, Shadow! Your friends are with you!"

You smile over your shoulder as you are pushed into the shadow of the king's massive stone keep. It towers ominously above you, and the wide, solid doors leading inside are slowly opened. Friends, you think. That's what got you into this mess.

So what's going to get you out?

Go to 72.

33

No, there's nothing you could possibly say or do to the guards that would help Keela or yourself. You'd just get yourself into trouble, and that's exactly what you don't need.

You walk slowly through the bazaar, blissfully ignorant of the merchants calling out and displaying their wares. The guards ignore you as you pass through the gate and enter the forest on the other side of the drawbridge. You are nothing to them, just as you feel insignificant to yourself.

You betrayed a friend to save your own neck. Face it, you're a thief. You constantly live on the edge of what's right and what's wrong, and you try to balance it all out in the end. But this time you went way over the edge, and a friend of yours will have to pay for your cowardice.

You go off the path, into the woods, to think in solitude.

88 MICHAEL ANDREWS

In a glade, you sit up against a tall oak tree and gaze at nothing. You're there for a while, but no matter how you try to look at it, how you turn it around in your mind, you cannot make yourself out to be a good friend unless you do something to help her.

You stand up and wipe the dirt off your pants. You have to go back. You have to try to redeem yourself.

You run back on to the path leading to the castle, but the sun is just going down over the horizon, and you hear the weights and pulleys in the castle gate as they drop the portcullis, and the castle closes for the night.

The gates crashes down with a final thud, and the drawbridge is hoisted up by its heavy chains. "No!" you scream into the sunset.

But it is too late. You friend is somewhere in captivity, where you may never be able to help her, and you will never be able to show your face in the realm again without being branded a traitor.

You turn away and head for your hut in the deep woods. You'll get a good night's sleep, that's what you'll do; then you'll pack up and move on to another realm far, far away, where you might be able to make a more honorable living, where no one knows you, and you won't have to live with their stares and accusations ever again.

But will you ever be able to live with yourself?

The End

34

"Wait a minute," you say. The second clue of the Arnstadt spirits suddenly comes to you, the one about "the two that were once one." And what was it that the cleric told you in King Halvor's treasury? You snap your fingers and smile. The cleric had said, "The jewel from the stars and the talons from the earth are the keys both to undeath and to rebirth."

You do not know what all of it means, but the crystal skull is supposed to have come from the stars, and the silver tip on this walking stick is in the shape of claws—talons. Perhaps these two things belong together, and Lord Fear did not even know it.

You tell Dare to stand close to the pedestal. He takes one side, and you push the staff's silver tip toward the skull.

"Careful," Keela says. "Don't move too fast."

The claws penetrate the energy barrier around the pedestal, then the silver claws touch the crystal skull. The room goes white with a burst of power. You blink to dispel the light from your eyes, then your vision clears and you stare at the scene before you.

The skull is on its side, blown over by the explosion. There are four small holes in its base.

The clawed tip of the walking stick has changed. From the clawed fist it was before, now the talons are open, and the claws gleam sharply in the light.

You smile. "I think we're doing something right."

You push the staff closer to the skull, closer, until the claws are almost touching the crystal.

Then the talons flex of their own accord, and the claws twist until their points are embedded in the crystal's four holes.

The skull glows with increased power. Slowly, you pull the staff and skull back toward you, and the three of you stare at the prize you must take back to the king. The two that were once one. Surely, the king will be pleased—

The dungeon of Lord Fear vibrates with angry energies. A mournful howl erupts from the floor, reverberating through your very soul, and the obsidian pedestal cracks and shatters, crumbling into a heap of black shards.

The howling dissipates through the castle. "A magical alarm," you say suddenly. "I started something when I took the skull." You pause and look sheepishly at your friends. "I hope I didn't wake something up."

Dare says, "Let us make haste and return to the realm."

"As quickly as possible!" Keela says.

You open the pouch and slide the completed staff inside. You tie the drawstring, and together the three of you run for the door.

Go to 48.

35

You do not really know why the thought came to you, but, for some reason, you think the king might enjoy seeing the black gem sparkle in the moonlight streaming through the castle windows.

You hold the jewel that had been Lord Fear between your thumb and forefinger, and you raise it above your head, holding it in a shaft of moonlight angling through the window. "Behold!" you shout triumphantly. "The evil wizard that had been Lord Fear is now—"

The gem begins to quake in your hand. You look up and see the jewel hungrily absorbing the pale moonlight, and glowing deep inside with a cold silver intensity.

You cry out and release the black gem, and as you do, the gem explodes with radiant energy, its black shards dissipating in the moonlight. . . .

Lord Fear stands before you, darkness swirling about him like a shroud of black mist. He screams with rage and spins on his heels.

"Halvor!" Lord Fear shouts. "You shall never have me, human! It is I who am triumphant tonight, released by your simpleton, the boy! And I will return to wreak my revenge on you and your house!"

Lord Fear begins to glow with a shimmering green light. He points a long, bony finger at you. "I shall return to take you as one of my undead, boy, when I claim the world as my own! Beware!"

His voice echoes away, like a nightmare receding into memory, and his evil spell corruscates around the lord of fear with flickering green energy, transporting him to a haven far from the warriors of King Halvor. You have no time to scream even "Noooo!" for Lord Fear, in a single instant, vanishes.

The king rises from his throne and stares at you, anger plain on his pale, fleshy face. "You stupid thief!" he shouts. "You had the villain where we wanted him, and you brought him back! He has escaped again! This is all your fault!"

You hang your head in shame. The king is right; if you had not been so stupid and foolish, Lord Fear would not have escaped. If the realm falls to the evil of Lord Fear, then you will be solely to blame. You don't know how you will ever be able to make this up to the king . . .

. . . but perhaps the king does.

"Shadow . . . Dare . . . Keela," the king pronounces,

"despite this unfortunate accident," he says, glaring at you, "you have proven yourselves worthy of my generosity, and have completed the quest I sent you out upon.

"Now I charge you with a quest far more dangerous. Before, it was simply to find a thief and return to me the crystal skull. Now, the threat of Lord Fear's revenge hangs over our realm. Your quest is to find Lord Fear and defeat him once and for all.

"Do this, and the realm will always be home to you, the bravest warriors of the land. Fail, and the fate of the realm will be on your heads."

The king stares directly at you.

You swallow your pride and apologize. "It is solely my fault," you say to the king, "and I promise that we shall find Lord Fear wherever he hides, and we shall rid our land of his evil for eternity!"

In moments, the three of you are assigned quarters within the keep. You need a good night's rest from your travels, for at dawn, in the purifying rays of the sun, you will leave once again on the trail of Lord Fear.

You lie down and close your eyes, letting sleep wash over you. Fear clearly had enough power to conquer a village, and he was amassing his undead armies for an asault on the realm. Now, bcause of your mistake, somewhere in the world he is waiting, planning. His powers are still mighty, and his mind so twisted with evil that you know he will never rest until he has his revenge on the realm—on you, for he will not rest until you are one of his undead slaves.

In the morning, you will start out again to recapture the lord of fear. Your path will be long and frought with terrors from the Abyss, but you will not rest until Lord Fear is found and dealt with permanently.

This is your quest . . . a quest that may last you for the rest of your life.

Good luck, Shadow. . . .

The End

36

The guards at the castle doors look you and Keela over, disdain and scorn plainly evident on their faces. The captain proudly tells them who you are and how he captured you, and they grin mischievously, their eyes twinkling. "So it's the infamous Shadow," one of them says. "Well, you ruined the king's ball. Now I guess you're going to get what you deserve." He laughs, and the other guard opens the castle door.

Your guards shove you and Keela inside, pushing you in the back. You stumble forward through the long halls of brick and stone, passing torchlit halls decorated with lush tapestries and ancient furniture. Then the guards halt before a huge set of double doors. "Wait here," the captain says to the guards holding Keela. "The king wants to see this one," he says, nodding toward the female thief.

"What? Where are we going?" you stammer. You did not expect to be separated from her.

With a mighty shove, the burly guard pushes you away from Keela and toward a small door down the corridor. With a black iron key, he opens the door. Inside, a staircase is lit by a single torch, and the stairs lead deep into darkness. You know where this staircase will take you.

"I don't want to go down there," you stutter. "Look, I'm sorry for starting a fight. I was just trying to—"

The guard pushes you, and the two of you start down the shadowed stairs. "I don't care, thief," he tells you. "No one gets away with punching me in my face." He shoves you again, and you stumble down three or four stairs.

His laughter echoes in the cold, dark stairwell. You come to the bottom of the stairs, where a single, thick wooden door awaits you.

"It's the dungeon for you," the guard says, laughing. "Oh, eventually, I'll tell the king that I captured you." He pauses. "Maybe. But right now, just remember who you hit. Just you remember who has the last laugh now."

Go to 26.

37

No, you don't feel very sleepy at all. Despite how bone-tired you earlier felt from the strenuous events of the day, you feel too nervous, too awake, to get much sleep tonight. Maybe it's this place; maybe just being in this deserted village is making you nervous.

"I'll take the first watch," you say. "I don't think I can sleep at all tonight. It feels like something is just . . . wrong here."

"I know how you feel," Keela says, "like we're being watched or something. But I need to be wide awake and alert in the morning, when we start searching again for Lord Fear. Then we'll make that dark wizard wish he had never thought of taking the crystal skull."

"Aye," Dare says, yawning. "Brave words, thief. But let's keep our thoughts of revenge until the morning. Wake me in three hours, Shadow," he says to you. "I'll take second watch. Maybe you can get some sleep then."

Your friends curl up on their bedrolls, and you put some more logs on the fire to keep the chill night away. In seconds, Dare is asleep and snoring quite loudly, and soon you see Keela's chest rising and falling regularly in deep slumber.

You know that, logically, you should feel exhausted after your long journey and the terrifying events in Carnivex Mansion. But you feel too restless to even consider laying your head on a pillow. You stand up and walk around the tavern, examining the few decorations on the walls: a landscape showing twin mountains and a long, rushing waterfall, and a shield bearing the symbol of an owl in flight, flanked by a black dagger on the left and a white dagger on the right.

You sigh and pace, but you can only look at the same decorations so many times, and you eventually realize that you've been pacing around the inn for over an hour. Bored, you walk over to the window and look out at the empty village street. All is quiet on the other side of the glass, and you impulsively decide to step outside and make sure that all is well throughout the village of Arnstadt.

The street is quiet, and the cold night sky is clear. The stars twinkle silently, like jewels flaring with crystalline energies, and a cold breeze blows down the street like a breath from an unhallowed grave.

Unexpectedly, you yawn. You think back on the events of the day, and soon you find yourself yawning repeatedly, struggling to keep your eyes open. You reach for the door to the inn, then you notice something out of the corner of your eye.

You step out into the street for a better look.

There, in the distance, across the village square, the light from a single candle flickers weakly in the window of a shop.

Someone is in there, you think. Someone alive! We must have missed him when we searched the village!

You look back at the forms of your friends, sleeping quietly on their bedrolls. Your watch is almost up; maybe you should get back inside and get to sleep, and you can investigate the light in the morning, with the others.

But something insde you is restless, still craving a little more adventure. What harm would it do to walk across the street and find out who lit a candle inside that shop?

If you go back inside the Red Room Inn, go to 21.

If you must investigate the candlelight, go to 73.

38

The ghosts' warning was clear: "Seek not to disturb these bones, or cursed be ye."

But mystic warnings never stop a dedicated thief. There has to be a reason an old, dusty coffin would be chained tight and hidden in a secret underground room. And the only reason you can think of is unimaginable wealth—the family fortune of the Arnstadts, hidden, not in a treasury or vault, but in a secret room guarded by the dead.

You enlist Dare for his help, and he smashes his broadsword down upon one of the coffin's padlocks.

The ancient lock springs open, and the warrior hammers the other two locks until they lie in pieces on the floor.

The chains fall loudly into heaps on the stone as well. You shove the warrior aside, and Keela watches over your shoulder as you push up on the lid of the coffin.

The old hinges creak in protest. In the fluttering blue light of the will-o'-the-wisp, you peek inside the coffin, but see only darkness. You lift the lid more, slowly, the rusted hinges screaming, and the blue light catches on twin orbs, reflecting coldly, like gems.

"They're here!" you cry. "Jewels!"

Then black mist spews from inside the coffin, swirling and billowing beside you in thick, dark clouds. You step back, momentarily surprised, and the mist reaches out for you with a smoky black tendril.

You smell it, then: a rotten, ancient smell, the fetid breath of the grave. Twin orbs glow banefully at you from within the mist as a hand of smoke tightly grips your arm.

Then the mist spins like a tornado, coming together, and takes solid form.

The man standing before you is tall and gaunt, wearing billowing robes of black. His white hair stretches down his shoulders in a tangled mess, and his wide black eyes blaze at you, coldly reflecting the witchlight. His face is white and drawn, pulled across his skull like thin paper, and his pale hands terminate in long black nails that rake your flesh like razors.

He smiles, catching your gaze with his. His eyes are hypnotic. You can look only at his eyes, glistening, calling you, holding you in their icy grip.

You do not notice your friends screaming for you to run. You do not notice Dare attack the man in black, or how he is grabbed tightly by the neck and thrown helplessly, like a rag doll, to the floor. You do not see the others scramble madly out the secret door and up the stairs to escape. All you see are the man's eyes, transfixing you, then his smile as he bares his long, white fangs and brings them closer, closer, toward the long vein, pulsating with terror, in your neck.

You gasp once, then all you see is blackness.

* * * * *

You open your eyes and know hunger.

The vampire is gone. With your new, heightened senses, you can track his invisible footprints on the floor.

The world awaits you outside—a new world, a world where the sun will never shine, where blood pulses like sweet, thunderous music.

For you are one of the evil undead now, a vampire.

And completely, utterly, alone.

A pang of loneliness hits you. Now you will never know love. You will never again see a sunrise. Never again will you feel heat, or know the meaning of friendship.

Your quest is over, and the search for the skull will go to someone else now.

Or Lord Fear will claim the world for himself and spread darkness over the land.

It does not matter to you. The world does not matter; your friends do not matter. The coldness of the grave is your constant companion now, your only companion. And all you will feel, for eternity, is an endless hunger, an incessant craving for blood.

He is out there—you can feel him—the one called Vertaal. You have loosed an ancient evil on the land, an evil, you know instinctively, from a dark plane known as Ravenloft, a plane of dark magic which now has spread to you....

You laugh. Shadow. What a good name for a vampire.

You lick your lips and feel the sharpness of your new fangs. You start up the stairs of the Arnstadt crypt.

The night world awaits. . . .

The End

39

Should Dare try for the skull, or should you waste time and examine the pedestal and the gems? You shrug. Let Dare see if there is a trap. It won't hurt you.

"Go ahead," you say. The warrior grins. "Spoken like a real man!" He reaches for the crystal skull.

The skull flares brilliantly with light, and Dare is thrown back against the wall, tossed effortlessly by an invisible force. He stands up carefully and shakes his head to clear his vision. His eyes appear crossed. "I shouldn't have done that," he says quietly.

Go to 52.

40

You reach out casually, keeping your eyes on your companions, and your fingers brush the golden rope around the edge of the pouch. You twirl your finger rapidly so the rope is wound around your knuckle, and you lift the pouch from the pile and bring back your arm. In a single swift motion, you slip the pouch into your pocket, and you follow the others out of the vault, no one the wiser.

The cleric turns and whispers an ancient word toward the vault. You strain to hear him, but his voice is too low. He turns and faces you and the female thief. "I earlier protected the vault with a spell that would alert me if certain valuable items were stolen, such as the king's ceremonial crown, or that crystal wand near the door." He looks at you. "It seems the realm can trust you thieves after all. Perhaps we will see the safe return of the crystal skull."

You look away, almost in shame. You don't know why you took the pouch, really. The cleric seems to think it isn't valuable—he did not even protect it with a spell. Come to think of it, you don't even want the little thing.

But there was something about it, something almost . . . important. It was as though it called out to you, like a whisper in the dark, yearning for you to take it. Your fingers touch the soft velvet pouch in your pocket, and it feels warm to you, as though it truly belongs there.

You're not sure why you took the pouch, but perhaps it will come in handy later on. And you wish you would soon get an opportunity to see if anything is inside.

The cleric closes and locks the vault door, then crosses his wrists and stands before the doorway. The hall is filled with his resonant voice as he speaks in a tongue unknown to you. "*O'Makana! Kanamaka! Hai! Hai!*"

His voice turns to thunder, and the hall is filled with swirling lights as they spin down in a vortex of light and power, then coalesce within the doorway to the vault, forming an impenetrable shield of magical force. The guards resume their places before the door, and the cleric steps back, weary from the effort of casting another spell. He takes a deep breath, then leads the way back up the stairs.

As you climb the moldy dungeon stairs, the cleric begins to speak, and you feel a chill fall over you and wrap its spidery tendrils throughout your chest. Just the very mention of the true thief's name is enough to send a cold stab of terror into your heart.

The cleric's words echo off the dank walls. "Lord Fear," he says, "is a most dangerous adversary. Once the trusted captain of King Halvor's Red Dragons, Lord Fear defeated his friend, the warrior Dare, and betrayed the king at the Battle of Wubur.

"Then Lord Fear—or, as he was still known then, Nevill

Carnivex—disappeared for several years. We knew nothing of his whereabouts until the village of Meriwether was almost destroyed by an army of the undead. It was Carnivex who had returned to the realm, with conquest as his goal and the restless undead as his servants.

"In the secret years, Carnivex had become a student of the dark wizard Teraptus, and had forged a bond with the forces of darkness for power and might. He relinquished his humanity in return for the soulless power of the night, and he claimed as his royal title Lord Fear, Prince of the Undead.

"Now, it appears, Lord Fear has decided to take the place of Teraptus and command the forces of darkness himself. If it is truly he who now holds the Crystal Skull of Sa'arkloth, then the realm is in far more danger than we ever expected. For if he knows how to control the skull's untapped powers . . ."

The cleric trails off, and you see him shudder speechlessly in horror. You can well imagine the terror that Lord Fear could unleash over the realm, for you have heard tales of the survivors from Meriwether, and how their fretful dreams are haunted by piercing red eyes and screams in the night.

You shudder once, hoping you never have to face one of the evil undead in combat. Then the cleric reaches the top of the stairs and opens the door, spilling blissful, golden light on you from outside in the hallway. You smile, secretly happy to step out of the darkness of the dungeons and into the light.

The cleric leads you and your companions to the main gate of the castle. There you discover that the king has ordered horses and supplies for your group, and you mount your steed in a single leap over its rump.

Dare nods appreciatively. "Well done, Shadow," he says. Even the cleric smiles. The others mount their horses and turn them around to face the cleric.

"These are some of the king's finest mounts," the cleric tells them. "You shall ride Flame," he says to the female thief, "a thoroughbred from the east that has proven to be one of the fastest horses in the realm. Warrior, your horse is called Arrow, for he has the uncanny talent to dodge the weapons of the most deadly foes. And, Shadow," he says to you, "your steed is named Bentley, after the eastern village where the crafting of fine weapons has been made into an art. Your steed will run like quicksilver and will carry you from danger wherever you find it."

The three of you are silent as the cleric raises his hands to the sky and blesses you. When he is finished, Dare asks, "Where do we ride?"

The female thief turns to him. "We have no choice. We must find the lair of Lord Fear and steal back the skull."

"But where does Lord Fear dwell?" Dare asks.

"With Teraptus gone, we are not sure," the cleric says. "But we believe he is maintaining his ancestral estate, Carnivex Mansion. It lies to the north, over the border, in the Forest of Shades."

The horses snort at the mention of Lord Fear, and your companions rein in their mounts before they bolt. You look at each of them, then say, "Let us ride."

The cleric steps back and raises his hand. "Farewell, avengers. May the Forces ride with you, and may your quest bring you back with the sun."

Dare takes the lead, while you allow Keela to ride in the middle. You plunge into the forest, where the sun casts freckles of calm yellow light through the canopy of leaves overhead. A short distance from the castle, Keela holds up her hand and calls a halt. You ride over to her while Dare doubles back.

"You know, perhaps there is an alternative to encountering Lord Fear so soon," she says. "I know of a wizard in these woods who may be able to locate the crystal skull using his spells and charms. If he can find the true thief using his magic, it might save our lives."

"You could be right," you say. "We don't know for sure that Lord Fear and his servants took the skull."

The warrior frowns. "I say nay. The evidence in the vault was enough for me. The cowardly Lord Fear is behind this, and we must find out where he has hidden the skull."

He and Keela look at you for guidance.

If you stay on the road toward Carnivex Mansion, go to 64.

If you decide to seek the wizard, go to 29.

41

You shrink back in your chair for fear of being seen with her. If a guard or a "concerned" citizen were to see the two of you together . . .

"Go away!" you tell her. "Go back to your friends and leave me alone!"

A look of dismay crosses her pretty face. "Shadow, what—"

"Are you deaf?" you whisper between clenched teeth. "I don't need to be seen with you! You can get me into trouble—"

"Oh? I can? You mean, more trouble than you're already in?" She stands up, anger blazing like fire in her eyes. "What kind of a friend are you? All I was trying to do was say hello, and that you did a good thing the night of the ball."

She leans down into your face, her voice filled with fury. "You may not know it, disappearing for months like you did, but you made the king realize that he had made a mistake imprisoning the peasants in the dungeon. He apologized to everyone in the land—except to you. Of course, the Carnassia family insisted that a bounty be placed on your head for the theft of the emerald collar, but the king was secretly willing to look the other way— unless he was forced to keep his word."

She rises and looks down into his face. "I wonder what you'd do if someone reported you to the king, hmm?

Maybe then you'd be crying for a friend, instead of turning them away."

"Look, I didn't mean—"

But it is too late. Keela spins on her heel and walks away, angrily jerking open the tavern door. She looks back at you, her eyes narrowed into angry slits, then slams the door shut.

Well, that could have gone better. Now, half the people in the tavern are looking at you and whispering to their companions. You'll be spotted for sure, and you can count on word getting back to the palace. It's time to get out.

You throw a copper piece on the table for the serving woman, and you push your way toward the door. At the bar, Jaim stops you. He places a hand on your shoulder. "Watch your back," he says. "It might be safer for you around here next month. Give it a little more time to cool down."

You nod and walk out quietly, squinting at the sunlight outside. You close the door, and the familiar sounds of the tavern fade behind you, to be replaced with the shouting and bartering of the bazaar. You enter the maze of tents and stalls, casting your gaze suspiciously at everybody. A woman taps you on the shoulder, trying to sell you fresh fruit from Coranthia. A bearded merchant near you shouts out, "Swords! Blades made of the purest steel! Let Akbar the Swordmaker hammer for you a blade beyond compare!"

You hurry away to the end of the market. There! Only a few more steps, and you'll be at the drawbridge that will take you to the safety of the forest.

There is a sharp cry behind you, and you hear the stampeding footfalls of running men. Too late! you know instinctively, and you make a mad dash for the open gate, toward freedom.

Behind you, there are loud cries of "Stop him! Catch that thief! It is Shadow, the thief!"

Your heart is hammering, and you are gasping for breath. You are almost at the gate when the opening is blocked by the shapes of two guards, Harveth and Ygar. You stop short and pant for air. Ygar steps forward with his spear and points it at your chest.

You feel a spear point jab into your back, and your arms are roughly pulled behind you while a guard snaps heavy iron shackles around your wrists. Ygar looks down at you and laughs. "Harveth was right," he says. "You're not in the castle for an hour, and you've already caused trouble. I guess we gave you all the rope you needed."

The guards turn you around and pull you toward the market, where many of your friends stand, watching you being led off to a long fate in the royal dungeon. Your face grows hot with embarrassment; you've really hung yourself this time.

Then there is laughter. You look up and see the female thief, speaking with one of the Red Dragons. He hands her a small pouch. She pours its contents into her hand, and you can see sunlight glinting off at least a dozen gold coins. She looks at you and smiles, and the guard thanks her for her loyalty to the crown in reporting the criminal known as Shadow.

Then a guard shoves you from behind. You stumble ahead, toward the keep and the long staircase leading down to the bowels of the castle. "Move along, thief," the guard growls. "It's the dungeon for you, so you better get used to it. Say good-bye to the daylight."

Go to 26.

42

You cannot pass up the opportunity to steal something right out of the king's vault. That statuette looks valuable to you, as it appears to be made of pure gold. It is only about three inches tall and appears to represent a god or a mythical warrior. But you know that the statuette will bring a lot of money on the black market—money that can be used to feed a lot of people in the poorer sections of the realm.

As the others file out the treasury door, you move quickly and palm the statuette in your hand like a magician. You pretend to scratch your neck and drop the golden figure down into your tunic, which is bulky enough to conceal such a small item.

You look up and pass through the doorway. Good, no one noticed a thing....

Your head suddenly reels with pain and the golden statuette burns against your flesh like fire. You scream out and fall to your knees as your companions gather round to help you. You feel tears running down your cheeks and scramble to pluck the statuette from inside your tunic.

It burns the palms of your hands as you cast it to the floor, and you relax against the wall as the pain subsides.

The warrior reaches for the statuette. "No!" you shout. "Don't touch it! It burns with unholy fire!"

But Dare already has the statuette in his hands, and he holds it as though it were no hotter than its normal temperature. "I don't know what you're talking about, thief," he says. "This is not hot at all."

"I don't understand," you say, weakly. "It burned my skin." You lift up your tunic, and a red welt the size of the statuette is glowing on your stomach.

The cleric takes the figurine and places it back in the vault. He closes the door and locks it, then casts a spell that protects the door from all intruders. Then he turns to you. "When the theft of the skull was discovered, I placed spells on many of the more valuable items in the vault, such as that statuette and the king's scepter and crown. It would cause the thief to experience burning pain, and would alert the palace that a thief was again present."

The cleric shakes his head and frowns at you. "You are a disappointment, Shadow. I thought you would honor your king by your service. Instead, you have shown that you can never be trusted." He snaps his fingers, and two treasury guards come over and lift you off the floor. Your wrists are placed in iron shackles. "Take him to the king," the cleric says.

The cleric, Dare, and Keela accompany you back to the audience chamber of King Halvor. He listens to the cleric's report of your wrongdoing, then stands and faces you.

"Your crimes against the crown have been many and frequent," the king says. "For this, you have lost your chance at freedom and redemption, and you will not go unpunished." The king's voice booms out across the chamber so that all may hear his proclamation. "Kir Trelander, known as Shadow, you are hereby sentenced to life imprisonment in the royal dungeons! Never again may you see the sun or sky, and may your name never again be spoken in public! May the Forces have mercy on you!"

The king sits in his throne and absently waves a hand. "Take him away."

The guards drag you from the chamber, toward your fate.

Go to 26.

43

With Dare and Keela behind you, their weapons raised high, you reach for the brass handle on the door to the right. Slowly, you turn it, and the latch bolt draws back smoothly. "It's unlocked," you say over your shoulder.

You ready your short sword, take a long, deep breath, then hurriedly swing open the door.

You rush in, your friends directly behind.

Indirect sunlight casts a gray, lonely pall over the room. It was at one time a study. A long desk, marred with deep gashes from a heavy axe, lies overturned on the floor. The walls are covered with floor-to-ceiling bookshelves of the finest wood, and what few books are left have been tossed haphazardly onto the floor, or thrown like trash on the dust-covered shelves. A globe of the world sits in its hacked wooden base, long ago sliced into hemispheres by someone's sharp, spiteful blade. Written in blood across the main continent—the land of your birth—is the word "MINE."

You look over the book titles and notice that there are no tomes on magic or the black arts—Lord Fear must have kept those for himself. But these other remnants of his all-too-human past have been left behind, worthless to an ambitious, evil sorcerer such as he.

It is a shame, you think, for you can imagine having a study like this in a palace of your own, filled with all your favorite books, which you can dive into and relive over and over at your leisure.

Ultimately, you have come to learn, evil is both stupid and cowardly. If Fear is now a lord of evil, then he must also be a lord of fools.

Dare single-handedly turns the desk right side up. Keela rummages through its broken drawers while you and Dare check the bookcases and floor for secret doors or treasure troves. But there is nothing to be found here, save for a geography book that focuses on your world.

You sigh and look at your companions. "Should we try another one?"

Dare nods. "Let's get this over with."

"Aye," Keela says. "I want to leave this place as quickly as we can. There's a . . . smell . . . about it."

You agree, for you noticed the sickly sweet smell as you first came into the house. It is the odor of rotting wood and mold—but underneath that, permeating the land and the house's foundation, is an undeniable stench of evil. . . .

"Let's go," you say.

Go to 25.

44

The ghosts' warning was clear: "Seek not to disturb these bones, or cursed be ye."

But mystic warnings never stop a dedicated thief. The coffin bound with chains is too risky, you think. Perhaps the chains are keeping something from getting out.

No, the treasure must be hidden within the stone coffins. There has to be a reason that three sealed stone sarcophagi would be hidden in a secret underground room. And the only reason you can think of is unimaginable wealth—the family fortune of the Arnstadts, hidden not in a treasury or vault, but in a secret room guarded by the dead.

You approach the sarcophagus of Franklin Arnstadt, the family patriarch. "This one," you say. "The jewels will have been entrusted with the head of the family."

The thief looks at you askance, then the three of you slide the sarcophagus's stone lid to one side.

In the blue light of the will-o'-the wisp, you see an ornate coffin inside. Carefully, you reach down, looking for hidden traps or springs inside the carved, stone tomb.

But the sarcophagus is safe, and you happily place your hands on the edge of the coffin and lift.

A green cloud of air rushes from the coffin and permeates the secret room. Keela staggers away, coughing, and Dare covers his face with his cloak.

A small glass vial had been placed in the coffin when the body was buried. In time, the vial's seal had deteriorated, and the mixture inside was released into the coffin.

But you broke the coffin's seal and took the brunt of the gas. It burns the back of your throat, and you cough violently, trying to expel it from your lungs. A perfect trap, you think, staggering back against the wall. It kills the violators of the tomb better than any ancient curse.

You feel a weakness in your joints, and suddenly you fall to the floor, your skin taking on a greenish hue. Keela collapses beside you, and Dare struggles helplessly against the effects of the gas, then keels over.

You cannot move your fingers or any other part of your body. You are paralyzed; you could not even scream for help if anyone else were around to hear you.

Then you laugh to yourself, for you realize that this gas was not meant to kill, but to paralyze anyone who tried to rob the Arnstadt tomb. You would not be dead, but more like the undead: a living corpse, until you slowly die of starvation. There is no hope, you think. No hope at all.

You lie there for hours, feeling as though you are going mad in the prison that has become your body. As the hours wear on, night fades away and you see sunlight angle down the crypt's staircase and filter into the secret room. You suddenly think that this is the last day of your quest, and that you will never recover the skull for the king. Your name will be remembered with ridicule throughout the realm.

Night falls again, and with it comes a chilling dread of Lord Fear and his undead. What if they were to find you here, alone in the darkness. The witchlight disappeared with the coming of dawn, and your friends are as helpless as you.

You feel warm tears trickle down your face, and you know you will never be saved.

Daylight filters into the crypt once again. Your stomach aches with hunger, and your immobile muscles are screaming with tension, yearning to move.

You are dozing uneasily when you are jolted awake by a bright point of pain suddenly blossoming inside your head. The room spins, howling with a churning, violent wind. You are suddenly dizzy, and your stomach clenches involuntarily. You close your eyes in pain.

The wind dies down, then disappears. Your stomach relaxes, and peace and cool air wash over you in a sweet breath. You look up, and you are in the audience chamber of King Halvor.

The king looks down at you from his throne. "Your spell has worked, cleric. They have been returned. But I do not see the crystal skull!" he announces angrily. "Your two days are up, thieves! What has happened?"

No one can answer him. You cannot even move to signal for help.

The cleric rushes from his place on the dais and examines the three of you in turn, paying attention to the green tint to your skin. Finally, he says, "Your Majesty, they have been subjected to an alchemical mixture. They are paralyzed, my lord."

The king rubs his chin. "Can you do anything for them?"

"Yes, Your Majesty. If I may have but a few minutes in my chambers, I can concoct a gas that will reverse the effects of the paralysis."

The king gestures for the cleric to hurry. You are left on the cold marble floor, your breast filled with a warm feeling of hope.

In ten minutes, the cleric returns with three cloths and a bottle of a blue liquid. He pours the liquid onto a cloth, then places it over your mouth and nose. As he does the same for the others, your throat tingles with a cool, minty taste, and your lungs seem to shiver as the chemicals permeate your body.

Your eyes blink, and your skin feels as though it is being pricked with needles. Then you can move your fingers, and your arm, and in minutes the three of you are up on your feet, the paralysis gone. You bow before your king.

Go to 68.

45

The front doors are sealed with some magic device, and the undead warriors of Lord Fear are coming closer, torchlight shining dully off their ancient blades. You can fight them, but you'll lose precious time if more of them show up and attack. No, maybe it will be better to try to get out of there through one of the other rooms.

The closest room is the drawing room, and you instantly remember the large, broken window opening on to the forest. You shout, "Come on! We have to get out of here before it's too late!"

Dare picks up the charred remains of a chair and tosses it at the encroaching undead. One skeletal warrior goes down under the chair's weight, then fumbles to get back up on its fleshless feet. The warrior has bought enough time to start toward you, and Keela joins you in a mad scramble for the drawing room.

You pull up short at the drawing room doors, for the torchlight illuminates the pale, ghastly faces of ten more undead soldiers marching through the room, toward you and your companions, the only living things in this mansion of fear. Their sockets glow with bloody light, and their disjointed, crumbling bodies lurch awkwardly forward, driven by the beating of your hearts.

"Over here!" you cry, and you back away toward the closest door.

Then the door splinters outward, and another group of the undead appears from the darkness and closes in on you.

You are surrounded by twenty or thirty of the undead. Perhaps you should have fought them when they numbered only four. Dare screams a battle cry and dives into them, his mighty broadsword hacking indiscriminately through bone and skull and decomposing muscle. But the forces of the undead are too many. As Dare goes down under the claws of half a dozen corpses, you are grabbed by countless undead hands and dragged away from the wall. Keela begins to scream in uncontrollable terror, and the teeth of the undead warriors sink deep into your flesh, seeking to satisfy their endless, unnatural hunger.

Your eyes begin to lose their focus, but you can clearly see light: the scarlet light burning hungrily in their eyes, and the golden light of the torch, now at your feet.

It is your only chance! You jerk your arm away from a corpse and pluck the torch from the floor. The drawing room door is open, and you cast the torch into the darkness as hard as you can.

The pain throughout your body is cold as you are dragged under by the undead. You dimly think that you failed in your task, but in moments the drawing room is lit by an orange glow, and you know that the torch has set the curtains on fire, as you had hoped.

You pray that the fire will catch throughout the house. You know that you will soon be done for, and you do not want to return to this world as a mindless minion of the undead.

The fire spreads through the drawing room and into the great hall, where the remnants of tapestries and curtains flare up to finish the bonfire that died prematurely, so long ago.

You smile. The others are dead, you are sure, and coldness is spreading throughout your body as the undead feed. As you succumb to eternal darkness, all you can think about is how you have saved your friends from an unholy, eternal fate.

Then the chill of darkness is turned into the raging heat of purifying fire. You hear the screams of the cursed dead as Carnivex Mansion blazes with the fires of righteousness, and as you are taken by the flames, your soul is saved from the undying curse of the undead.

You die a hero.

The End

46

You think back on the night's events and realize just how exhausted you really are. You've had enough for tonight, you think, and you're not ashamed to tell them.

"This crypt will still be here in the morning, and Lord

Fear will still be hiding up in the castle. Why don't we wait until dawn and get started then? There's no sense in exploring now—or fighting any more of the undead—if we can hardly stand up for lack of sleep. I'm so tired I could barely defend myself. What do you say?"

Keela agrees with you, and Dare, who is always ready for a good fight, finally comes over to your side. The three of you start back toward the village.

The moon is sinking below the horizon by the time you return to the village square, but there is more than enough light to see that your horses are gone from the post where you tied them earlier.

You race over to the front of the Red Room Inn and examine the post. The tethers are torn or snapped, and the dirt road shows signs of heavy trampling.

"They bolted," you say, analyzing the clues. "It looks like something scared them."

"It must have scared them a lot," Keela says, "to make them snap their leather reins. Look at their hoofprints! They must have been going mad!"

The ground in front of the inn is a jumble of crescent-shaped craters, and you can dimly see three sets of hoofprints leading down the road, out of the village and back toward the forest. "They headed for the Forest of Shades. I've never known a horse to get so frightened—"

Dare whips the sword from his belt and points into the tavern. You and Keela spin around. In the red glow of the dying firelight inside, shapes are moving, casting flickering shadows against the walls.

"I'll go first!" the warrior says, and he crashes through the inn's wooden door without hesitation.

You jump in behind him, then almost collide into his back. "What is it? Why aren't you fighting them?"

Then you see for yourself who the intruders are. A dozen armed warriors of the undead turn to face you, interrupted in their task of searching for you. Their eyes glow wickedly, and as one they start toward you, their whitened teeth glinting coldly in feral smiles.

Keela runs out first, then you are immediately behind her, tugging on Dare's cloak. He spills out almost on top of you. Gasping in terror, you point in the direction of the graveyard, where at least two dozen more undead are shambling toward you. "We don't have a chance!" you cry out. "We can't defeat this many of Fear's slaves!"

The thief tugs on your elbow. "Our only chance is the forest!"

"No!" the warrior shouts. "We must stay and fight like the king's champions!"

You and Keela start running toward the village gate. "There are too many! Come on! You will live to fight another day!"

The undead crowd through the tavern door, and Dare backs away, then turns and speeds along beside you. Together, the three of you run without looking back.

Your run into the forest is a blur. You do not stop until you are deep into the woods, panting raggedly for breath.

The Forest of Shades lies between the village of the undead and Carnivex Mansion. In the dark of night, you have no idea where to go next, so the three of you climb up the largest trees you can find and decide to wait out the night in their wide, protective boughs.

In the morning, you wake, achy from your uncomfortable perch high above the ground. But at least you are alive, and there is no sign of the undead.

Your party starts off down the road toward the mansion, hoping that no diabolical traps have been set for your return. There, you can take the country road back to King Halvor's realm, where perhaps you can find a farmer or journeyman who can give you a lift to the castle.

By noon, you reach the edge of the forest, and Carnivex Mansion stands silent before you, like a sleeping dragon. On your signal, the three of you race out of the forest for the country road, only to find that there is no need for caution here. No traps await you, and the road seems clear and safe.

You walk through the forest for the remainder of the

day. Just before dusk, you discover a cool stream. You decide to camp there the rest of the night, then start on in the morning. Dare goes off, then returns later with some game to cook over an open fire.

Your night in the forest is restful and quiet, but you long for the comfortable security of the castle. In the morning, you wash yourself in the stream, then start again on the road toward the realm.

However, you have forgotten the edict of the king when he set you upon this quest. Not an hour down the road and away from the evil of Carnivex Mansion, the world suddenly begins to spin. You and the others fall to your knees, suddenly hit with a bout of dizzying nausea. Your eyes go dark, and your head rings with the fury of buzzing insects.

Then peace and cool air wash over you in a sweet breath. You look up, and you are in the audience chamber of King Halvor.

The king looks down at you from his throne. "I do not see the crystal skull!" he announces angrily. "Your two days are up! What has happened?"

Go to 68.

47

You look up the dark stairs. Lord Fear is probably up there; wizards always have their chambers on a tower's top floor, you think. But you're not ready to face Lord Fear. It may still be daylight, but a wizard like Fear is powerful all the time.

The open doorway under the stairs beckons you: perhaps it will lead you to the crystal skull's hiding place. You point with your sword. "Let's look through there. We'll go through the rest of the keep later."

Keela lights torches on the walls and hands them to you and the warrior. You pass through the open doorway and step into a short hall. One door opens onto a pantry of cleaning supplies. Another door is open at the end of the hall, and leads you into the library.

Here, the half-empty shelves hold only books of forbidden magic and ancient lore. All other books have been taken off the shelves and strewn around the room like garbage. Apparently, Lord Fear has a liking for only books that can help him along his dark path.

A set of double doors in one wall is closed. Dare bravely opens them without worry, and you step into the next room.

Go to 51.

48

You turn the sharp corner of the narrow passageway and start running up the long flight of stone stairs leading to the alchemistry laboratory.

Halfway up, you stumble to your knees. The world has suddenly gone cold and dizzy, and the steps look longer than they really are.

You look back at the others. They are faltering up the steps, the same as you. You are all struck by a curious, unnatural vertigo; your depth perception wavers, making distances appear short at first, then long.

You climb slowly up the stairs on your hands and knees. Your eyes cannot be trusted, so you climb using your fingers as your eyes, reaching for the next step toward daylight and safety.

Finally, your fingers tell you that you are on the small landing that leads to the laboratory. You shout, "I'm at the secret door! Come on! It's only a little way more!"

Then you open your eyes.

The laboratory is moving. Your vision will not focus, and it looks as though everything in the lab is swimming in slow motion.

The others appear at the secret door, and together you start on your long journey across the laboratory and up the stairs to the king's chamber.

But you have never been on a journey as long as this. A single step in the right direction takes longer than you can imagine. It feels as though are are walking at the bottom of the ocean, and you know now that when you took the skull off the pedestal, a maddening spell was released that somehow slows the march of time for you and your companions.

And you realize with horror that if every step takes five or ten minutes, then you may not be out of the castle by nightfall.

And the servants of Lord Fear will then surely discover you.

Finally, after seemingly hours later, you are across the lab and at the base of the spiral stairs. You look up and gasp, for it looks as though the stairs are pumping up and down, slowly, like a giant spring. You close your eyes again and reach out with your fingers. Crawling by touch is the only way you can retain your sanity.

Minutes pass by, then hours, perhaps even days; your distorted senses can no longer tell a second from a decade. Inexorably, you make your way up the curving stairs, constantly trying to fight off the nauseating waves of terror in your stomach.

Then your fingers fall upon a cold stone floor and you are in the foyer at the top of the spiral stairs. You stand awkwardly and open your eyes, but your vision and senses are swimming murkily as before. "I'm at the top!" you shout, but you have no idea if your friends can understand you with their senses as distorted as yours.

You feel a hand grasp your ankle, and dimly you make out Keela. You help her to her feet, then grasp Dare's hand as he takes the last few steps up. How long did helping him take? A few minutes? An hour?

How long do you have left?

The going is straight from here, through the sitting

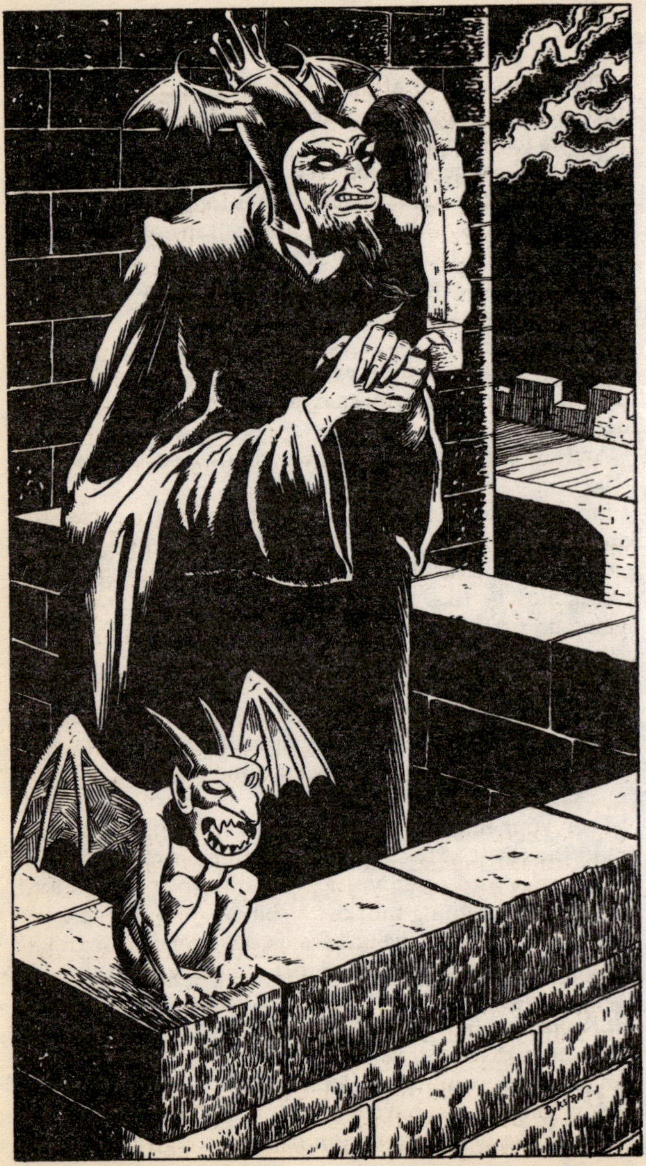

room, the ballroom, then the foyer. You have no idea what time it is, but you know you must hurry, else the undead rise under cover of night.

You crash through the double doors into the sitting room. The doors to the ballroom seem miles away.

Your heart is racing like a horse's gallop, and cold sweat beads your brow like a fever. You feel as though you've been running for days, yet you are not even halfway to the doors.

Keela stumbles. It takes you a day to go to her and help her up, and a week to start running again for the doors.

Finally, a year later, you get to the double doors. They open at your touch, and a century later you are still running through the ballroom for the exit, the doors leading to the foyer and to the blessed daylight.

Laughter. You hear echoes of laughter bouncing off the walls around you. The sound of it chills your blood, and you pant for breath, doubling your efforts to escape this pit of terror.

Then you are at the doors leading to the foyer. You are almost outside. You push on the doors . . .

And they are locked.

Your whole body rings with evil laughter and vibrates uncontrollably. You fall to the floor with the others, stricken with violent shaking as the spell leaves you and is drawn away in a rush.

You lie there on the floor, gasping for air like a dying fish. Normal time has been restored, and you feel the world around you the way it should be.

You glance up.

They surround you, an army of darkness. Their shields are rusted and broken, their swords scratched and dented with age. Little flesh hangs off their bones, and their eyes gleam with crimson, unholy light.

A chuckle emanates from the end of the room. A tall man approaches. His undead muscles ripple beneath his thin skin of pasty gray flesh. His eyes, sunken into their shadowy sockets, glow with an unhealthy, feral light. The beard at his chin is cruel and jet black, stark against his long ebony hair streaked with silver, and upon his head is a tall black crown from which springs the wings of a bat and the skull of some dead thing.

He laughs, and his laughter is the sound of the tortured wind. "I'm so glad you could make it tonight," he says, his voice rumbling like the tremors of the earth. "I am the lord of this humble abode."

He laughs again, loud, like the crackling of thunder.

"Welcome, foolish mortals, to Castle Fear . . ."

Go to 6.

49

The door is identical to the other doors in the great hall, made of thick, ancient oak that may have withstood a century of use in this mansion. Its huge hinges are of black cast iron, and the handle is of tarnished brass, gleaming dully in what little sunlight is coming through the front doors. You look back once, wishing you were outside and finished already. Sundown is only a few minutes away.

Keela nods at you silently and gestures toward the closed door, as if to say, "Go on, let's get this over with." Dare readies his long sword, balancing the blade before him.

You shove open the door and jump in, your short sword out before you.

Dim light filters through heavy drapes closed at the far end of the room, and another tall window is directly across from the door, its glass shattered. Beyond you can see a ragged line of trees at the side of the mansion. Around you, you can dimly make out several chairs and couches, their cushions ripped apart. Other chairs and tables are overturned or broken throughout the large, comfortable room that was formerly the mansion's drawing room, where guests and residents long ago met to play games or simply talk in a setting far less formal than the living or dining rooms. The room is lorded over by a huge marble fireplace angled in one corner, large enough for a man to stand in comfortably. The interior of the fireplace is relatively clean, and it stands out starkly against the wanton destruction that Fear has left throughout the rest of the mansion.

The three of you begin your search, righting some of the couches and feeling through them for anything hidden in the stuffing. While the warrior knocks on the walls, looking for secret doors, you peer behind slashed paintings and tapestries for doors or any other hidden clues; but all you find are bare walls and spiderwebs. No secrets here.

At the rear wall, Keela pulls aside the long drapes hanging from the ceiling. Dingy sunlight slants through a wall of thick glass, and behind it you see what used to be a conservatory, filled with brown and withered plants creeping up the walls and roof, and spreading out through broken panes and through a doorway, open to the outside, far in the rear of the greenhouse.

A glass door is set in the transparent wall, and the thief tries the handle. "It's unlocked!" she says. "We should search in here, too!"

"Wait!" you cry. Your voice echoes around the room repeatedly, for you have stepped inside the huge fireplace in the corner. You sniff, and only the barest scent of soot wafts to your nostrils.

There is something strange about this fireplace, for although this mansion is at least a century old, by your estimates, this fireplace is unusually clean, as though it had rarely been used. Its placement here in the corner is odd, too, and something about it just doesn't sit right with you.

"What is it, Shadow?" Dare asks.

"It's a fireplace," you answer smartly. Dare frowns. "But that's not important. I think there is something here. There's something about this fireplace that is decidedly odd. Look," you say, gesturing. "The drawing room is always the most popular room in any mansion. All the family gatherings are held here, in summer or winter. But this fireplace shows almost no sign of use. No soot, no ashes. No scorch marks on the stone." You run your hand across the smooth, clean marble at the back of the fireplace.

"Like the blackened marks on the walls in the great hall," the female thief says.

"Right." You step out and face your friends. "If they didn't use the fireplace to have fires, then what did they use it for?"

The warrior waits silently, lost in thought.

"I'm not sure about anything right now, Shadow," Keela says, "except that we might have just enough time to search one more place, then we better run out of here before nightfall. Who knows if Lord Fear is still around or not?"

You nod in agreement. The skull could very well be hidden in the mansion's conservatory, possibly buried in the earth or in one of the numerous clay pots you can see through the glass wall.

On the other hand, what is it about the fireplace that obsesses you? Is something there to tug at your curiosity, or are you just imagining it?

If you decide to search the conservatory, go to 67.

If you decide to search the fireplace, go to 53.

50

"Why don't you sit down? I could use some company."

She looks you over. "Hiding out in the forest, huh?" You nod. "You look it," she says. "It looks like you haven't eaten for a year."

She calls to the serving woman to bring two heaping plates of beef and cups of wine. "This is on me," she says. "Our score at Ghurakta was all due to you."

She takes the seat next to you and leans in. Her strong voice is barely above a whisper.

"You really pulled a good one on the king," she says, a glint in her eyes. "I wish I had been there."

You try to remember who had been incarcerated in the dungeon with you. Come to think of it, all your fellow thieves had been rounded up and imprisoned . . . except for her.

"Where were you that night?" you ask.

She sighs theatrically, but you know that she loves to tell tales of her adventures, just as much as you love to captivate audiences with yours. "I know it sounds impossible, but I was on a mission for the king himself."

The king! You almost jump up from the table and bolt for the door. If she is in with the king, then you have no business being seen with her. Who better than a thief to know how untrustworthy thieves can be?

She notices your unease and places a hand on your shoulder. "Hold on, Shadow. You need not be afraid of me. I had sneaked into a banquet in the palace when we were attacked by Lord Fear and his death knights."

You gasp out loud. Lord Fear! He was once a powerful lord of the realm who embraced the wizardry of evil in order to gain more power. Rumors abound concerning the trickery of Lord Fear and the powers he holds—powers so strong that he can command armies of the undead.

"When Lord Fear and his death knights broke through the windows, I thought we were finished. They were in search of a wizard who had escaped from the evil mage Teraptus, and who came to warn the realm of the mage's evil.

"We engaged them in combat, and somehow we defeated the undead. Then we were charged with a mission to seek Teraptus and destroy the source of his powers: a Sunstone, which threatened to cast the whole land into darkness.

"I was questing with a warrior, the escaped wizard, and Greenthorne, an elf, when you enjoyed the excitement at the royal ball. When I returned, you were long gone, and your audacity was spreading like fire throughout the realm. So, tell me . . . what did you do with the gold tooth?"

"I gave it to a beggar on the outskirts of the castle," you say, laughing. "He needed a new tooth a lot more than that slob, Bleehall."

She smiles. "The king had no right to jail the poor in his dungeon. How did you escape the castle?"

"It made me furious," you tell her. "The king even had little children and families taken in, for fear they would disrupt his little party by begging.

"They treated us all right, though. The food was exquisite—I guess the king wanted to make up for what he knew was unjust imprisonment. But it wasn't enough. You can't buy someone off when you've done something wrong, and I thought someone had to show him that.

"I gave a scullery worker three silver pieces for his fancy banquet uniform, hat and all. Then, in a closet at the top of the dungeon stairs, I found some old horsehair paintbrushes and some varnish. I knew I'd be recognized once I got upstairs, so I pulled the brushes apart and glued the bristles inside the hat with a little varnish. The hat and the black horsehair covered up all of my own hair, and then I glued some short hairs above my lip to make it look like a moustache."

This is the first time you've told anyone what really happened at the ball, and you feel like you're finally letting go of a deep secret. You lean closer so no one else can hear.

"The guards let me out when they saw that I was just a simple server at the ball. I walked around for half an hour, serving treats and candies, pouring drinks for the lords and ladies. Then the Lady Carnassia made me angry, treating all the servants like slaves and peasants, ordering them here and there. She even yelled at one for spilling a drop of wine on her gown.

"So I got my revenge.

"It was barely fifteen minutes later when the Lady Carnassia screamed that her necklace was gone. Stupid cow! Hers was the first item I stole, and it took her a quarter of an hour to figure it out.

"As soon as she screamed, I was heading for the doors. I walked right out of the palace, gave some of the delicacies to the guards at the gate—with the king's compliments, of course, for doing such a good job at their post—and I walked right out. By the time the guards were alerted that a prisoner had escaped—a notorious thief known as Shadow—I, a lowly server, had vanished into the woods.

"I did not steal a lot from the guests, but I hoped it showed them that all people deserve to be treated with the same respect due the nobles of the land. And the trophies all went to good causes."

The female thief smiles appreciatively. "Well, don't worry about getting caught now. The bounty on your head was canceled last month." You gulp. A bounty? "King Halvor apologized to the citizens he had imprisoned, so maybe you taught him a lesson after all. Besides, the king has other things to worry about, things much more serious than the Lady Carnassia's jewelry . . ." She pauses and whispers softly. "Some are worried about the spread of sorcery over the realm."

"Sorcery?" you say. "What do you mean?"

She takes a swallow of her drink. "Thankfully, we defeated Teraptus, and light was returned to the realm. But lately, hints of evil have been detected throughout the land. Snakes have been found with three heads. Only a few leagues away, the Forest of Tolat was found empty. No birds, no animals. In the shade of the trees, the coldness was palpable, like a living thing. And the warriors who reported this said they could feel eyes watching them. They returned to the palace in haste."

You watch her silently. Perhaps these were signs of a new, powerful mage taking residence in the realm.

"Not even the king's closest advisors can explain these

things to him. All they can say is . . ."

The tavern door suddenly slams open and sunlight streams in, momentarily causing you to wince. The patrons quiet down, and you hear heavy footsteps enter the room.

Then you can see the men. There are three of them, Red Dragons, and they're walking by each table, scanning the crowd. "They're looking for someone," you whisper to Keela. "I knew I shouldn't have come back. It's me they're after."

You look down at your drink, praying that they will pass over you and go to another table. You feel their heavy footsteps in the wooden floor as they approach, then pause beside you.

You look up.

"Here's the one!" the guard cries. And he reaches down

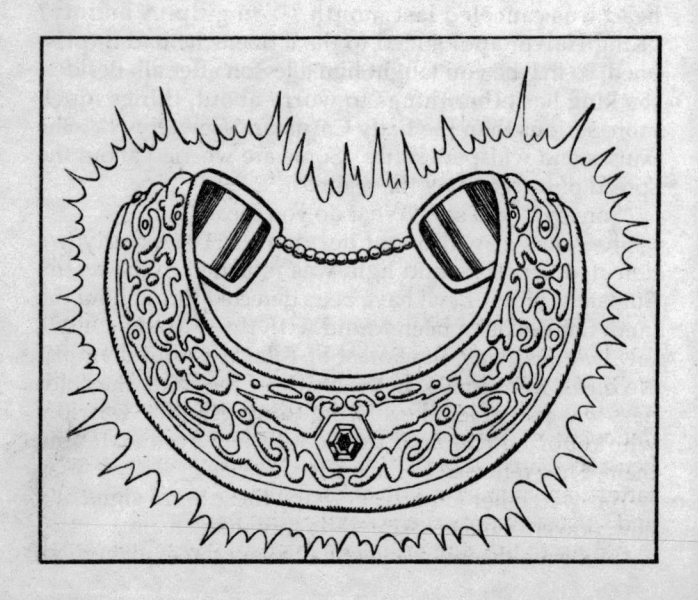

and grabs Keela by the collar.

"Hey!" you say. "She's done nothing wrong!"

The guard looks at you as though you were an insect. His face is fat and beefy, and his nose is twisted, obviously broken several times in the past. Keela squirms in his grip. "Let me go, you big ox!"

He laughs at her futile struggle. The other guards come over.

"You," the burly guard says to Keela, "are to be brought before the king immediately. You have been accused of a crime against His Majesty!"

Keela is in trouble. Maybe you can help her get out of it by defending her—she's been here talking with you, hasn't she?

However, defending her may prove pointless. You could help her escape by fighting with the guards, or you could do absolutely nothing. Let them take her away, and you can probably leave the castle without fear of being caught.

If you stand up for Keela, go to 32.

If you let the guards take her away, go to 14.

If you fight with the guards, go to 58.

51

You open the double doors and step into a huge room. The long marble floor stretches far into the distance. This is the castle ballroom, decorated with statuary and tapestries that now are stained with dust, or have been ruined deliberately by the sharp edged weapons. Dishes are broken and shattered across the great hall. Tapestries hang in tatters, and something that looks like blood is spattered and smeared across the once beautiful floor.

A door to the side leads to a kitchen, where the stench

of rotten food is highly present. In the far wall, another set of doors leads you into a short hall lined with old wood and hung with paintings representing the Arnstadt legacy—all of which have been slashed or torn apart.

Another set of doors opens onto an opulent chamber full of rich furnishings. This is the master's private sitting room.

Behind one of the long tapestries hanging from the ceiling you find a door set into an alcove. The door opens easily.

In the foyer before you is an iron door, set firmly into the wall. To the side is a set of stone stairs, spiraling down into the earth, perhaps to the dungeon, you think. Lord Fear has probably hidden the crystal skull deep under the castle, where he feels the most comfortable.

But the iron door looks like the entrance to the family treasury, and the chances are equally as good that the skull has been placed inside.

The choice is yours.

If you open the vault, go to 4.

If you go down the stone stairs, go to 60.

52

You shake your head in annoyance at the warrior. Cautiously, you step closer to the pedestal, feeling waves of power emanating from around the skull. "It is obviously protected by a spell of some kind," you say. "No, let's leave the skull alone for now. I want to look at these gems."

You scoop up a handful of the rubies and gasp. They are warm to the touch, and they hum in your hand, as though they are alive. You know you've got something special here, but you don't know what to do with them—if anything.

You frown. Something is tugging at the back of your mind. You think, trying to place it—and suddenly, it comes to you.

"The ghosts' clues," you say out loud. "The first prophecy has come true. We found the skull on a pedestal of power."

"Then this spell," Keela says, "is not on the skull itself, but protects whatever is on the pedestal."

The three of you are silent. While you're wondering what to do about the skull, you realize that something must be done with the gems. They seem too valuable to leave here, but you don't know if they are cursed, or dangerous, or even harmless.

If you put them in your pouch, go to 18.

If you leave the gems there, go to 61.

53

You look toward the dimness inside the conservatory and shudder involuntarily. Since the mansion was abandoned, many of the stronger plants have crept up the glass wall and spread across the conservatory like a grotesque spiderweb. A feeling falls over you like a cold shadow; you do not want to go in there. The plants just don't seem . . . right to you somehow.

No, you're sure that the three of you are better off right here in the drawing room, and that the fireplace holds a secret that only a crafty thief like you can uncover.

The mantle of the fireplace seems to have been carved out of a single, huge piece of the rarest marble in the world, imported from the southern continent of Kyrell. Its surface is smooth and cool to the touch, and you run your hand over it slowly, from the floor to the top of the mantle only inches above your head. "Nothing," you say.

Dare shifts on one leg and crosses his arms. "I want

some action soon," he says. "Just what are you doing?"

You glare at him. "The fireplace had to be used for something, or else it wouldn't be here. If it wasn't for fires, maybe there's a secret passage here."

Dare catches on and smiles. "Riiiiight. I get it."

You look up into the darkness of the chimney. You run your hand over the lintel, then along the smooth surface of the back wall. There are no cracks or hinges to indicate a door, and there is no latch or opening mechanism readily visible. Two metal andirons stand inside the fireplace. You shift them, hoping that one is a lever for the door you think is here. But nothing happens. To the left of the fireplace is a rack of fire irons. You touch the rack and try to move it, but the rack is fixed into the stone wall and is not a lever.

You take a step back and try to look at the fireplace as a whole, from the flagstones that form the inner hearth to the Carnivex coat of arms carved into the mantle. You close your eyes for a moment. You're trying too hard. You're looking everywhere for something that's probably obvious, right in front of you. You take a deep breath and relax, then open your eyes. You try not to focus on any one thing, but instead let your gaze wander, let it be pulled naturally to . . .

There! In the far right corner inside the fireplace you see a black smear of soot or ash staining the corner flagstone. "I need a light," you say. In a few seconds, you hear Keela rummaging through her pouch. Then a flame is struck and she hands you a burning twig for a few seconds of warm yellow light.

You nod in satisfaction. Up close, the stain is not soot or ash at all. It is a small hole hidden in the corner, easily overlooked as ash by someone less cunning than you. You poke your finger in it and feel nothing. Yet the torch affords you a glimpse inside the hole to see that there is something down there, like a plate of some type.

"It's a hole, probably a device, I think. I need a—"

You stop, for perhaps the very tool you need is waiting right in front of you. You take the poker from the rack and step inside the hearth. The tip of the iron poker fits neatly into the hole, and you jab it down deep inside.

From behind the fireplace, there is a soft click as a latch is released. You pull out the poker, and you suddenly hear wheels grinding and weights being sprung and lifted on hidden pulleys.

The back wall of the fireplace opens slowly, revealing a darkened passage. You peer inside but can see nothing at all. "We need a torch," you say.

Dare says, "I saw one out on the wall in the great hall. I'll be right back."

Keela bends down and looks inside with you. "What do you think?" she says.

"I don't know, yet. But I've got that feeling," you divulge to her, "you know, the one thieves get when they're on to something big." You can't help smiling widely. In the dim light, you can see by her own smile that she understands completely. "Something is definitely here."

The warrior returns with an unlit torch, and Keela lights it with her flint and steel. Dare enters the passage first, lighting the way.

The room is not very big, just room enough for the three of you. A spiral staircase of stone leads up into darkness.

Again Dare takes the lead and starts up the stairs. You and the thief closely follow the warm glow of the torch. The warrior stops to burn away spiderwebs with his torch, and you say, "This must go all the way to the attic. I'm sure we're on the same level as the second floor now, and there are no secret doors up here at all."

You continue the rest of the way in silence. At the top, the staircase ends at a small landing of stone. A simple wooden door is closed before you, and Dare reaches out for it. "Careful!" you say. "There could be a protection spell on it."

The warrior tests the door first, tentatively reaching out with his fingers for the telltale energies of a magical spell. "I feel nothing. There is no spell here." He reaches for the handle and says, "I hope." He opens the door.

The door creaks open, and the small room on the other side is lit by the torch's flickering glow.

A heap of chairs, boxes, wood, and books lies in the center of the room, ready for burning in a bonfire like the one in the great hall. A jar of flammable oil and several torches lie nearby on the floor. But it looks like someone forgot their duty, or was called away too soon. The shelves and bookcases around the room are still half full with curios and books. To you it looks as if this was a secret chamber for someone, a place where he could hide valuable items or do arcane research in privacy. Or perhaps this is where a prisoner was once kept by Lord Carnivex, or . . .

Face it, you just don't know the purpose of this room, except that things such as a stuffed weasel or a pair of deteriorating, winged boots were kept here. Perhaps, and most likely, now that you think of it, this was a storeroom.

You rub your chin. A secret storeroom. Then, if a storeroom is kept secret, that would mean that it's probably storing something pretty valuable. . . .

The items on the shelves are covered in dust and look ancient, worthless. Perhaps these things were valuable only to the Carnivex family, heirlooms and discoveries handed down through the generations. To you, it looks like none of the items are truly worth anything, nor do you detect a hint of them holding any magical qualities. Still, there's a nagging voice in the back of your head, telling you that there is something here in this mansion, and that it is up to you to find it.

"There is nothing here," Keela says, shaking her head. "A secret room full of trash. I can't believe we've ridden this far to find absolutely nothing."

"We shall find the crystal skull," the warrior says, sheathing his sword. "If it is not here, then we shall ferret out Lord Fear and take it from him by force."

The female thief looks at him incredulously. "Right. You and how many armies? Well, Shadow, we ought to get started. We're not going to find the skull standing around here." She turns toward the door.

"I'm not sure," you say. Keela watches you expectantly.

"I think we've overlooked something. For all we know, the skull—or something—may be right under our noses."

Keela scowls. "The only thing under our noses is that pile of trash," she says, pointing, "and I'm not going to play around through that. Come on. We still haven't looked through the conservatory."

You stiffen when she mentions the conservatory. Up here in the secret attic room, the evil that you detected in the greenhouse seems far away. You still do not want to go in there. Every nerve in your body is screaming "Don't do it!" But your own words come back to haunt you. "I think we've overlooked something."

Maybe you should ignore your feelings of dread and trudge back downstairs to the conservatory. There may be a clue in there that you will desperately need. Or maybe you should play a hunch up here and rummage through the trash pile in front of you. You don't know what you might find.

If you return to the conservatory, go to 24.

If you search through the trash pile, go to 27.

54

As you stare at the artifacts on the desk, the old man's words echo in your mind: "Pick one, the one you like better. And it's yours."

Your eyes flick back and forth between the crystal ball and the wondrous clock. Slowly, you reach out, first toward one, then toward the other. Without thinking, you make your decision . . . and your hand closes upon the golden clock.

The metal gleams brilliantly, the light shimmering across its golden surface like fire. The face is slightly yellowed with age, but the timepiece's hands are ornate, crafted with remarkable, intricate workmanship, and you can tell that the clockmaker must have been very proud of his handiwork.

You reach out a finger and trace the delicate scrollwork on the hands. The clock shows that it is almost two in the morning, but you are sure that the time is incorrect; it cannot be later than nine or ten at night.

You push the hour hand back to ten. A wave of dizziness rushes over you, and you look up to see the old man, grinning wildly. Through a dull, distant roar, you hear him say, "You don't have a chance against Lord Fear! Even time itself is his to command! Arnstadt—and then the world—will be his!"

Then darkness clouds your eyes, and . . .

Go to 37.

55

Your horse, Bentley, shies away from the imposing ruins of Carnivex Mansion. You can certainly understand why your horse does not want to get closer. Never before has your heart been so filled with fear as it is now as you stare at the dark house waiting for you.

You know your only chance for a normal life is to find the crystal skull and return it to the king. But your heart is racing like the gallop of a horse, and your palms are clammy with sweat.

Yes, the cleric had been weakened when he placed the spell of no escape on you, but you are so far from the king's realm now, perhaps the cleric's spell has dissipated with the distance.

You take a deep breath and hate yourself for what you're doing, but you simply cannot go in that mansion. You just can't!

Suddenly, you jerk your horse's reins around and Bentley tears away from the mansion at a brazen gallop. Behind you, your companions are shouting, "Shadow! Come back!" and "You can't escape, thief! You must help us find . . ."

But their voices disappear under the thunderous pounding of your steed's hooves, and you are enveloped by the pleasant peacefulness of the surrounding forest. Here, in the woods, you can make yourself a home far, far away from the realm and the wrath of King Halvor. Here you can live off the land, just as you did after you stole the emerald collar. You frown, thinking you will never be able to retrieve it from its secret hiding place in the king's castle, but then you smile ironically. Neither will anyone else.

You go deep into the woods and deliberately lead the horse off the forest path. Your companions might come after you, and you need to find a hiding place that no one will ever—

You shake your head. Suddenly, you feel dizzy. Pressure starts building inside your head like a swarm of insects buzzing to be released. You sway upon your saddle, and in an instant you find yourself squirming facedown on the ground, your body racked with dizzying pain. Your skin flushes with heat, and it seems as though you are spinning in a violent tornado of ashen wind that howls through your bones.

The wind becomes a scream, and you realize that you are screaming as well, in frenzied terror. Then the storm builds to a crescendo of power, like the haunting wail of a banshee, threatening to tear your mind apart with unstoppable force. Then, suddenly, there is silence.

The heat disappears from your body, and the wind dies away as though it were never there. You open your eyes . . .

. . . and you find yourself in the audience chamber of King Halvor.

The king is standing, watching you. You rise to your knees and hang your head in shame. The cleric approaches and snaps his fingers. Guards rush to your sides and clap your wrists in iron.

The king raises his hand. "You have attempted to escape, thief!" the king says loudly. "You were given a chance to redeem yourself, and you have failed! I only hope that Keela and my warrior can find the crystal skull without your aid, for by turning your back on the realm, you have turned your back on Keela!

"You will go now!" he says. "For violating your oath to your king, I sentence you to life imprisonment in the royal dungeon! May you learn your lesson in eternal darkness, and may the Forces have mercy on you, for you shall never be forgiven by the realm!"

The king dismisses you. The guards surround you and take you through the door into the hallway, where you are led to another door, made of thick, hard wood and bound with heavy iron.

Go to 26.

56

Your friends are out in the hall, probably looking for you. But you are so tired, aren't you? Wouldn't a nap feel great right now?

No! You have to force yourself to think, fighting off the sleepiness that has come over you like a spell.

You stagger away from the bed, groping like a blind man for the door. The air is cold and clammy on your skin, and the doorknob seems to be freezing in your hand.

You twist, but the knob won't turn. Somehow you've been locked in.

A twinge of panic flutters in your chest. Then you smell something, a perfume, sweet and light. You turn and stare at the bed, a pleasant smile on your face, and you yawn.

Go to 16.

57

"My lord," you say, "I think we should examine the scene of the crime, to discover any clues left by the thieves."

The king considers your request for a moment, then nods. "Very well. Cleric, you will take them to the treasury."

The cleric bows and steps off the dais. He motions away the guards and says, "Follow me."

You bow in farewell to the king, and the cleric leads you out of the royal audience chamber, Keela and Dare following close behind. You weave in and out of intersecting hallways lit by flickering torches on the walls. The cleric stops in front of a thick tapestry hung from floor to ceiling, and he pulls it aside.

The door before you is wide and thick, and the cleric takes a key from his pocket and unlocks it. Hinges creak, and torches light the way down a set of stone steps lead-

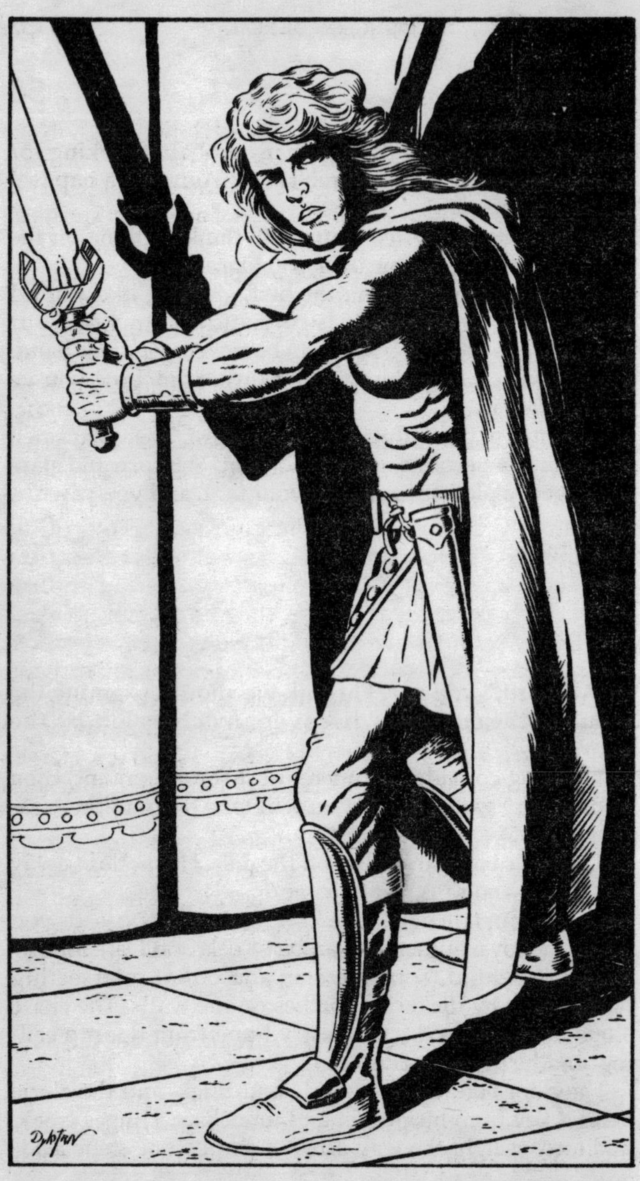

ing deep into the earth.

The cleric leads the way with a torch held high in his hand. You start down the steps, Dare at the rear. The air is cooler here in the dimness, and you can smell the dankness of the earth in these hidden chambers that have never seen the light of the sun.

The cleric suddenly speaks to you, his voice echoing off the barren walls. "The theft from the vault occurred the night of the attack by the minions of Teraptus. As your companions here can prove, Lord Fear and his undead servants attacked us in order to capture a mage who had escaped from the dark wizard. They were barely defeated—Lord Fear himself vanished before our eyes—and a party went out to confront Teraptus and dispel the evil darkness emanating from the wizard's castle.

"When the changing of the guard occurred in the morning, the sentries who had been at the vault during the night were found bewitched by a spell of endless sleep. Despite my best efforts, they have yet to wake." The cleric stops on the stair and looks in your eyes. "I cannot detect evil about you. I believe you innocent, Shadow, for neither you nor Keela could have cast such powerful spells. But I fear that it is your burden to prove your innocence, and perhaps bring the king's guards back to the world. For until the true thief is found, no one is safe."

The stair turns sharply, and before you lies a small room where ten armed guards are flanked in front of a heavy iron door set deep into the wall. "The vault has been sealed since the robbery was discovered. No one has stepped inside, and the treasury is more heavily guarded than before," the cleric says. "The king is taking no more chances."

The guards step aside as the cleric approaches the door. He crosses his wrists before him, and you hear him whisper, *"N'shug'orrath, litannus . . . vorteria notavius!"*

The door suddenly glows, protected with a spell of magical force, and the light emanating around the door swirls away in a vortex of shimmering energy.

The cleric opens the door. "The treasury was magically protected when the thieves broke in. Their powers must be great to effortlessly shatter a spell of mine."

You follow Keela and the cleric inside. Dare steps in behind you. You look at him curiously, and his eyes seem to narrow at you. "What are you looking at, thief?" he says.

You shake your head. "Nothing."

He comes closer to you. His face seems red with anger. "I know you have gained the trust of the cleric and the king, but you have to prove yourself to gain my trust. Keela has already shown herself to be a valiant fighter. You are nothing to me but a common thief—until you prove yourself worthy of my respect."

You swallow nervously, and Dare slowly turns his attention to the cleric. You take a few steps away and look around, silently in awe at the wealth surrounding you.

You are deep underground in the king's vault, and around you, on shelves along the walls and in tall piles on the dirt floor, are chests and boxes of shining gold coins, of gems and jewels and necklaces, of silver figurines, of crowns and goblets and wands and scepters—all the wealth of the realm, collected over the decades by the king and his ancestors, and secured in the vault where you stand.

The light glittering off the gold and jewels is dazzling. You have never before seen so much wealth, and your mind swims at the thought of what you could do with all this gold. You would never again have to steal for a living. You could share the wealth with poorer villages all across the land and ensure that the hungry and the needy never go forgotten.

The cleric walks over to a shelf against the far wall. There is a space between a set of solid gold candlesticks and a jewelry box made of gold and studded with rare gems. "The Crystal Skull of Sa'arkloth," the cleric begins, "was given to King Halvor's father over twenty years ago by the royal wizard Taurokkus. It was placed here for safekeeping, for the wizard knew that such a powerful item, if it ever fell into the wrong hands, could mean the doom of the realm.

"The skull was crafted eons ago from a crystalline star that fell from the sky and was discovered in the Valley of Stars. It is said to hold arcane powers that are unknown even today, and is said by some to have been delivered to mortals by the Forces, for purposes we can only imagine. But the first human ever to have used its awesome powers was a mage, Sa'arkloth, over seven centuries ago. Even then, the skull was legendary across the world, and the myths say that Sa'arkloth discovered the skull in the western lands, in a realm that had been decimated by forces unknown. Somehow, he rediscovered the skull's powers, and the land and its people were restored."

The cleric shakes his head. "Sadly, no trace of Sa'arkloth's journals concerning the skull has ever been found. We know only that the skull holds magic more powerful than any our wizards can control. Taurokkus, the first King Halvor's royal wizard, did battle with a black mage named KorLu, who claimed the skull and attempted to use it against the realm. KorLu was defeated, but the powers of the skull were great. Although the skull may be handled by nonmagical humans, no wizard can remain uncorrupted by its energies—that is why Taurokkus, in his wisdom, gave the skull to the king—for he could not allow it to fall into the hands of an evil wizard . . . and he did not even trust himself with it.

"Indeed," the cleric says, his eyes lighting up, "he used to speak of it only in secretive tones, and was fond of quoting a chant or ode of some kind, by an ancient poet. Let's see . . .

"'The jewel from the stars
And the talons from the earth
Are the keys both to undeath
And to rebirth.'

"And now the skull is gone," the cleric says, turning

away. "Its powers are said to be unimaginable." He spins suddenly and faces you.

"And the three of you have to find it. You must find it before it is used to destroy all that we know."

You think for a moment, scooping up a handful of gold coins and letting them run between your fingers like water. "Perhaps the thieves came to steal something worth only money, not magic. Perhaps they will try to sell it somewhere."

"No, I doubt that sincerely," the cleric says. "Look around you. No gold or silver is missing—only the king's most powerful item of magic. And when the crime was discovered, I cast a spell and detected traces of unnatural evil here in the vault. No, the thief broke in knowing exactly what he was looking for."

You nod, for the cleric is right. The thief that broke into this vault came specifically for the crystal skull, and he knew that it was a priceless item of untold powers. The thief came for the skull's magic, and not to make money off it.

You look up at the ceiling and all around you, along the shelves, behind them, between the piles of gold. Keela sits back on a stack of silver bars and stares off, thinking silently. Dare crosses his muscular arms in front of his chest. "We are doing nothing," he says. "We need to find some action and take revenge on the thieves who did this to King Halvor."

You smile at him, knowing exactly how he feels. You would like to see some action, too, but you have absolutely no idea what to do or where to go to reclaim the skull for the king.

You pace around the room, letting your gaze wander over the piles of wealth. Near the door, you stop and stare at something on the floor, a swirl of dirt and a shape embedded in the soft, earthen floor. A footprint!

"Look at this!" you say, and you get down on your knees.

The others come over and surround you, peering over

your shoulder. The female thief kneels on the floor beside you. You look at your friend with a smile across your face, for the footprints in the dirt floor are unmistakable. She looks up and smiles.

You say to the cleric, "No one has been in the vault since the robbery?"

"No one at all. The theft was reported after the guards were discovered unconscious. This is the first time that anyone has entered the vault."

You stand and look the cleric in the face. "This was no ordinary theft," you say. "Your thieves were the undead." You point at the footprints. "These prints were clearly made by the feet of a corpse." The cleric kneels down and traces imprints in the dirt left by a skeletal heel and the bones of a decomposed foot. "It looks to me like the attack on the castle by Lord Fear was a diversion. Perhaps they did want that wizard, like you said. But that was extra. They really wanted the crystal skull, and while everybody was upstairs fighting off the undead, at least two made their way down here and took off with the skull. Perhaps that is why Lord Fear vanished suddenly—he transported himself down here to claim the skull for himself."

Keela speaks up. "And that is why Lord Fear was not present at the castle of Teraptus to defend his master! He escaped with a prize of his own!"

The cleric strokes his beard in thought. "Your words ring true," he says. "I think that the king was very wise in allowing you to prove yourselves innocent of this crime. So, what will you do now?" the cleric asks.

You shrug. Well, there isn't much you can do. You can't exactly run off and attack Lord Fear, who probably commands a legion of the undead. The king's guards and Dare barely defeated the foul lord last time. No, you got into this situation to save your hide, not take unnecessary risks. But you have to try something. You have no choice. It's either the dungeon or Lord Fear.

"We must ride to the lair of Lord Fear," you blurt out. You look up, and your companions are looking at you with wonder in their eyes. "If he has the crystal skull, then what choice do we have? We must steal it back from him and return it before he knows that it is gone. Who better to do this than the finest thieves of the land?"

"Brave words, Shadow," the cleric says. He gestures for your group to leave the vault. "I hope you can make good on your boastful claim."

Dare leaves the room first, then Keela, who longingly looks back at the gold she knows she can never have. You stop at the door and hold your hand out like a gentleman, allowing the cleric to leave before you. He passes through the door, not suspecting a thing.

Now's your chance! All the king's jewels and riches have cast their spell on you, and you have the opportunity to quickly take something without anyone seeing.

On a pile of gold to the left of the door there is a small, golden statuette of some ancient warrior; a red, velvet pouch, fringed with a rope of gold; and a wand made of crystal, topped with a silver figurine of a woman with wings. Your eyes grow wide at the sight of such priceless treasures, and you're sure you can take something without anyone noticing.

If you try to take the statuette, go to 42.

If you try to take the pouch, go to 40.

If you try to take the wand, go to 1.

58

There is not much you can do, you're afraid. Inwardly you curse yourself. This is your first day back to the castle, and already trouble has reared its ugly head, looking straight at you. Well, discretion is the better part of valor, you've always believed. That's why you're a thief. You can slink in the shadows and run away, always hiding and striking quickly, then escaping with your loot.

But this thief is a friend of yours. You and she get along together beautifully, and you've got to do something to help her. It just doesn't look like being discreet will aid you in this matter. Perhaps causing some kind of a scene will afford both of you a chance to escape.

You stand up and stick your face into the face of the captain of the guard. "Just what is all this about?" you ask, deliberately making your face appear as enraged as possible. You can feel the anger building inside you, and all you can do is hope that the guard will back down, seeing that you're ready to do battle for Keela.

Maybe you made a mistake this time. Unfortunately for you, all the guard does is flinch as you shout into his face, and then his eyes grow wide and his large, round cheeks burn hot with anger. He is at least a head taller than you, and he leans down into your face, making you take a step back until you stumble into your chair.

"Is there a problem, little man?" the guard snarls.

Your noses are almost touching now. His breath is hot on your face, and you can smell that for lunch he ate something with garlic in it. No matter. You won't give up. You're in too far now. "Leave her be!" you shout. "She has done nothing wrong!"

Absently, you hear the patrons of the bar shouting you on. Taverns are the same all over the realm. Everybody loves a good scrap, and it's even better when it's a little guy against the authorities.

The guard's eyes narrow, becoming beady. They focus on you slowly, and a new light appears in them, the light of realization. "I know you," the guard growls, grinning. "You are Shadow! The thief of the collar!"

That's it, you think. There is nothing else to do but . . .

"Fight!" you scream, and your right fist is a blur as it swings around and pummels the guard in his cheek. The guard staggers back, surprised at your strength. But he stands up straight as the crowd begins cheering you on. His cheek is red where you hit him, and he suddenly lurches for you, his massive hands outstretched, ready to claim you in his iron grip.

You are smaller than he is, and much faster. You are already on the tabletop and leaping behind the guard as he reaches your chair, and in one swift move, your booted foot kicks out and shoves him from behind. His face goes down in your chair, then he jumps up, his eyes blazing, burning with the lust for revenge.

Keela kicks one of her guards in the leg and punches the other in the stomach with a quick jab of her elbow. The crowd roars with laughter, and the captain of the guard picks up your chair and heaves it at you.

You duck and roll quickly away, and the chair spins through the air and crashes into a table, spilling mugs of ale all over the customers. Instantly the patrons shout with delight, and the men drenched in their own drinks leap from the table and swarm toward the guard.

You look at Keela as the tavern customers all rise happily, ready to join in a good fight. Your eyes plead with her. Now! Now is the time to escape!

She nods rapidly. The fights begin as you scurry under the tabes, aiming yourself toward the door. A boot accidentally lashes out and kicks you in the thigh, but you pay it no mind. This is exactly what you had hoped for. Let everyone else fight to their heart's content. You've got to run away.

All around you chairs are crashing, drinks are sloshing on the floor. The patrons shout curses as they battle each other for no good reason, and you weave your way toward the door through a maze of tables and chairs and broken glass.

Then you are almost at the door. You rise, ducking quickly as a pewter mug comes sailing toward you to crash through the tavern window. Keela yells, "Come on!" and holds the door open for you. You take a step toward her, then a shape rises from below to block your way. It is one of the guards who had held Keela, grinning sillily at you. His fist flies toward your face, and you have no time to duck. The impact on your jaw hurls you off your feet, and you come to an instant later, sprawled across a tabletop. The guard grabs you by your tunic and spins you onto your stomach. In seconds, iron shackles are locked around your wrists, and you are picked up and placed on your feet.

Keela has been shackled as well, and with their free hands the guards unsheathe their swords and call for order.

The fighting around them subsides, save for a knot of men in the center of the room. Suddenly, the men are thrown upward, as though by an explosion, and the captain of the guard bursts from the tangle of men, his face crimson with rage. He bellows, "Stop this now, in the name of the king!"

Quiet reigns in the Rose and Crown. The captain shuffles across the ale-soaked floor, kicking chairs out of his path as he makes his way to you. He grabs your face in his hand and squeezes. You wince at the pain in your jaw. That guard may have broken it.

"You are the cause of all this trouble, Shadow. And so help me, I'll see you pay."

He turns you around and kicks you out the door. You fall to the ground, spitting sand and bits of dirt from your tongue. Then the guard hauls you to your feet, and you and Keela are shoved forcefully toward the dark, ominous towers of the castle keep.

Go to 36.

148 MICHAEL ANDREWS

59

The stairs to each side of the hall lead up into a gallery of shadows. Wizards' chambers are usually in one of two places, you think: at the lowest part of a building, or at the highest. You see no doors or stairs leading downward, so you point your short sword up the stairs. "There. Lord Fear's quarters will be at the top of the castle. It is there we will find the crystal skull."

Keela lights three torches on the walls and hands one to each of you. You start up the stairs, seemingly protected by the glow of the flames—but you know that this aura of protection is only illusory.

On the second floor, you find a curving hallway that seems to circle inside the keep. Closed doors are on each side. You open one to find a linen closet for palace guests.

Another door opens onto a study, where guests can enjoy some quiet time in the castle.

The other doors are bedrooms, decorated with ornate furnishings and ancient paintings. Over it all hangs a patina of dust, reflecting the months of disuse during which Lord Fear has dominated the region.

The warrior goes on ahead while the thief tries doors on the other side of the hallway. You cannot find stairs that lead to the upper floors of the tower, so you figure they must be somewhere else on the first floor.

You grab the doorknob of the next door, but you do not notice the coldness in the metal. The door opens easily, and when you stick your head in for a cursory search, your eyes instantly focus on a painting of a beautiful woman. Her long, light brown hair cascades down over her pale shoulders, and her eyes are the most beautiful green you have ever seen. The portrait's eyes captivate you, pulling you into the room almost against your will—but you are completely willing to look over this portrait.

The door closes softly behind you. You are so haunted by the portrait's face that you do not hear the door lock itself, nor do you notice a cold breeze as it passes from the door to circle the room, as though it is looking you over.

Her eyes gaze at you knowingly, as though the two of you have known each other forever. The brass plaque on the painting reads

---

ANGELINE
BELOVED WIFE

*"That your eyes may haunt me
forever should be the curse of love."*

You wish you did know her. Her lips appear so soft, so inviting, and her eyes are as wide and warm as the ocean . . .

It is obviously a woman's room you are in. The soft, comfortable bed is canopied by a fine, diaphanous fabric, and the decorations are all distinctly feminine. You yawn, suddenly tired. It is a little chilly in here, you notice, and the covers on the bed certainly look soft and warm to you.

You yawn again. It is hard to keep your eyes open. A nap would feel nice right now. Your companions won't even notice you're gone. There is nothing here that can possibly hurt you, right?

You blink suddenly, and you realize you are crawling into the bed. You've forgotten something . . . Lord Fear! That's it! I've got to help them find the skull before Lord Fear discovers us!

A cold wave of sleepiness hits you, and the thought of danger evaporates from your mind. Lord Fear just doesn't seem all that troublesome to you, just a big, harmless shadow. But a nap would feel wonderful, wouldn't it? Just climb right into that bed and sleep, sleeeeepppp . . .

You force your eyes open. You know you shouldn't sleep, but it is hard to resist.

If you take a nap, go to 16.

If you leave, go to 56.

60

The vault door beckons quietly with promises of wealth, but you have never seen a castle treasury that has not been hidden well. No, you think, this looks like a trap.

Anything in this castle may be a trap now that Lord Fear has become master of the domain, so you motion silently to your friends and proceed carefully down the stairs.

The spiral staircase leads far down, under the castle. The torches seem to cast little light down here where darkness holds sway, but it must be your imagination playing tricks.

At the bottom of the long staircase, a wooden door stands ajar. Dare bravely pushes it open.

The room inside is an alchemist's laboratory, a sanctum sanctorum for wizards experimenting with their magic. One wall is filled with shelf after shelf of old, leather-bound books, parchment scrolls, and talismans the likes of which you have never seen. Another small bookshelf is against a stone wall, and arranged before that is a series of lab tables, holding vials and bottles and philters used in alchemical experiments. The three of you go over every inch of the laboratory, knocking on bricks, searching behind books.

It is Dare who stumbles upon the latch hidden in the small bookcase. As you are an expert, you look it over for traps, then carefully push the latch until it snaps.

The bookshelf comes away from the wall, and you open it to reveal a narrow staircase carved into the stone. The air here is cold, and your nose wrinkles at a stench that you can only define as the stench of evil.

"This is it," you whisper. "This has to be the hiding place of the crystal skull. I know it."

Silently, the three of you file down the narrow stairs, careful not to slip on the moist, slick mildew. At the bottom, the passage turns sharply. Dare takes a deep breath, then suddenly leaps around the corner and disappears.

You and Keela look at each other, fear glistening in your eyes. Like the warrior, you take deep breaths to steel your nerves, then you jump around the corner.

The torchlight plays along the walls like sunlight rippling across a pond. The object in front of you seems to absorb the light and cast it out in waves of energy. It is the Crystal Skull of Sa'arkloth, transparent, sculpted from a single piece of unbelievably pure crystal.

It is more vibrant, more beautiful, than anything you ever imagined, and you can understand how thieves and mages could lust after it so. Its eye sockets hold huge rubies, glimmering by torchlight, and its shimmering crystal teeth seem to smile at you in a frozen rictus of incomprehensible laughter.

Is it laughing at you, or does it seem to be laughing at all the tragedy it has brought to the world?

The skull is situated atop a shining obsidian pedestal, and around the pedestal, piled in careless heaps, are hundreds of identical, small rubies, all the size of a fingernail.

Dare approaches the pedestal, his goal clear in his mind. You can feel power in this room, power emanating from the area of the skull. "Hold on," you tell Dare. "This thing may be protected by a spell."

Dare laughs. "I am fed up with magic tricks. Let us get the skull and leave now. King Halvor and I can return later with his armies, and we can tackle Lord Fear when he is unprotected by the power of Sa'arkloth."

He looks at you angrily. "Come on! Decide!"

If you let the warrior try for the skull, go to 39.

If you examine the gems, go to 52.

61

You look at the seemingly harmless gems, then at the beautiful skull, and you realize that even tiny, pretty things can be dangerous, too. You toss the gems back onto the pile and no longer care how priceless they appear. They could kill you. You look at the skull. "Now what do we do?"

"I'll try and get it," Dare says. "I'm sure I can withstand anything this spell can put out."

"No, no," you say. "Lord Fear is behind this spell, and his power may know no boundaries. No, let us think."

You place your hands on your hips and glare at the crystal skull. It is protected by a spell of blind energy around the obsidian pedestal, and you have no way to grab the skull and run. If only you had something with which to push it off the pedestal. Then Dare could catch it and you could get out long before darkness falls and Lord Fear discovers the theft.

You look around but spy nothing that could help you. The hand on your hip brushes the pouch you found in King halvor's vault, and you remember what you placed in there, the thing you found in Lord Fear's home.

You open the pouch and stick your hand inside. It is cooler in the infinite realm contained within the pouch, and your hand closes on the walking stick you kept there. You pull it out and look at it.

Go to 34.

62

You pass hurriedly beneath the huge portcullis and mingle into the crowd milling through the castle market. Merchants and vendors from all corners of the realm have set up stalls and tents here. To your left, one stall is filled with cages holding rabbits, snakes, mice, weasels, and all manner of small animals. One cage, ornately decorated with gold and silver, holds a black cat. As you glance at it, the cat leisurely spreads its white, furry mouth and yawns.

To the right, an old woman, dressed in flowing robes of black and crimson, holds up a pendant of silver. It swings in a circle above a wooden square that is filled with sand, and the crone shouts out, "Your future! All your fates shall be revealed by the sands of time! All your futures, for one low price!" The woman sees you, and a glimmer of recognition sparks in her eyes.

You wave and put a finger to your lips, and you merge with the jostling crowd.

You know most of these merchants. You were practically raised here in the market, and you are familiar with all the ins and outs of the king's bazaar, and all the sellers and their wares.

More importantly, they know you and like you. You are a familiar sight throughout the realm, and tales of your outrageous exploits have spread across the land.

As you enter the bazaar and blend in with the crowd, you frown in thought. If one of the king's guard had somehow seen easily through your disguise at the spring pageant, then your fellow citizens—some of whom you trust, most of whom you do not—certainly also know of your alleged escape at the royal ball. And some may be willing—for the right price—to inform less tolerant authorities than Harveth that the notorious Shadow was seen in the bazaar, and that the thief of the emerald collar could be had ... perhaps for only a thin gold coin.

You feel their eyes staring at you, piercing you with their cold gazes. You think they are friends ... but perhaps they are not. You duck and weave through the crowd, claustrophobia bubbling unreasonably in your chest, pounding like a hammer. Perhaps you're overreacting. Perhaps you have nothing to fear from your friends and acquaintances.

But can you be sure?

You shove your way through the peasants and nobles, hiding your face. The crowd thins somewhat, and ahead of you a sign swings above a very familiar oaken door. It is your favorite tavern, almost a second home to you. If there is any place where you can be sure you are safe, it is under the sign of the Rose and Crown.

You sigh in relief and open the door.

As you step over the threshold, your nostrils are assailed by the heavy odors of pipe smoke, of baking bread, of spilled ale on the wooden floor. The patrons' voices are raucous and ring loudly in your ears. You push your way past a burly merchant guzzling a mug of ale at the bar. He looks down at you and nods. "Shadow," he says merrily. "Haven't seen you in these parts lately, m'boy."

"Jaim," you say, recognizing the farm merchant. "Nice

to see you, too. But let's pretend you never saw me today, all right?"

He smiles. "Yes, the climate still seems a little hot at the castle, doesn't it? Ever since the night of the ball . . ."

You wave uncomfortably and move quickly past him toward the back of the room. You hear his laughter as you walk away. The bartender, Nash, spies you and nods once, knowingly.

An empty table awaits you at the rear of the tavern. There the torchlight is dimmest, and from that vantage point you can see everyone who enters the room.

Well, you never expected this. After stealing the emerald collar straight off the Lady Carnassia's neck, you figured that two months of hiding in your hut in the woods would take off some of the heat. Already, you fear, half the people of the realm have seen you, and word is probably on the way to the palace that the infamous thief of the royal ball has returned to the castle.

Coming back so soon may have been a bad idea.

But a man's got to make money, right?

Nash sends over Jaan, a serving woman you know. You're nervous from your run in the bazaar, and all you order is a tall glass of cold water to help you cool off. You'll have something to eat a little while later, when it's closer to nightfall, and after you've relaxed a bit.

Laughter erupts from a table in the front corner. You look across the room. A wiry little warrior is cackling with laughter over some joke, and his companions are chugging their drinks and calling out for more.

A woman gets up from their table and turns toward the bar. You recognize her sandy brown hair, the confident swagger in her walk. At the bar she orders more drinks for the table. She's a thief, too, and a friend of yours. Last year, she aided you in an adventure in the mines of Ghurakta, where you made off with four bags of diamonds. The minekeepers had worked your cousin and his family to the bone in those mines, and your escapade there helped your cousin's village. You smile at the memory.

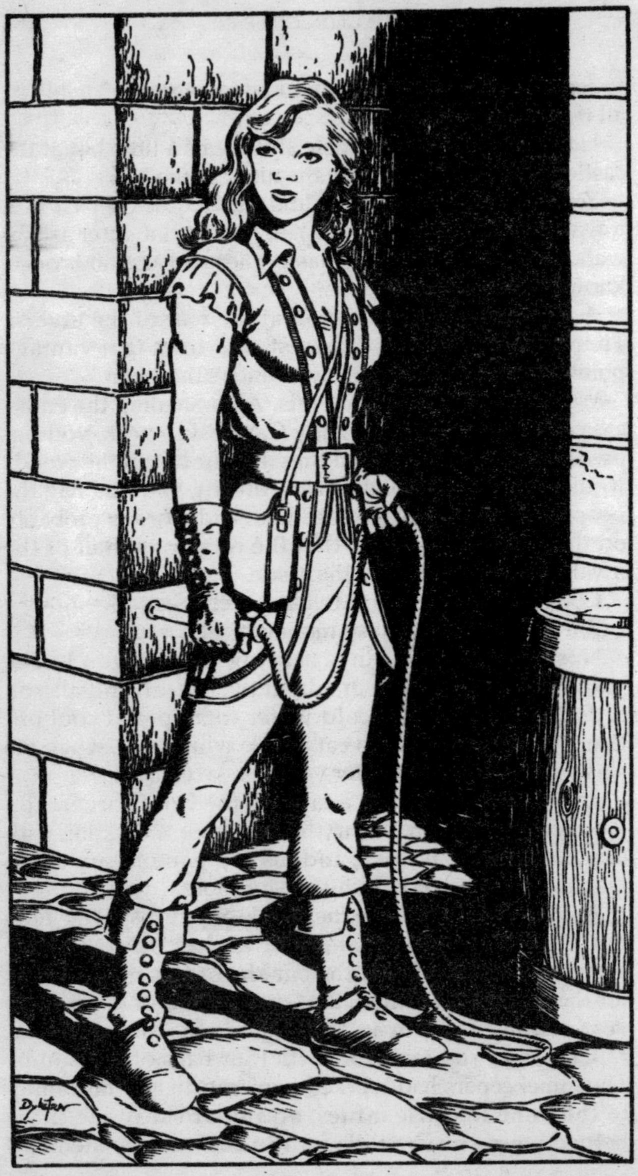

Not only did your adventure result in the mines being closed due to the minekeeper's cruelty, but your share of the gems put food on the table for the entire village.

And the mines had been owned by the Carnassia family.

Keela turns at the bar and sees you alone in the back. She raises her hand. "Ho, Shadow!" She takes the drinks to her table, then makes her way back to you. "The famous Shadow. I never expected to see you around here again. I thought you had run off to find your fortune in more hospitable climes."

You shake your head. "No, I never left. Maybe I should now, though, after the welcome everyone is giving me."

She watches you expectantly. Your table is empty, and you realize how lonely you have been for the last two months. She's Keela, isn't she? Perhaps you should invite her to sit with you for a while. Maybe she can tell you if it's safe for you in the realm or not.

Then again, you don't want to cause any suspicion. Two thieves huddled together at a table might look like a conspiracy to others.

If you send Keela away, go to 41.

If you invite her to sit down with you, go to 50.

63

You take a deep breath and momentarily think of your friends asleep in the Red Room Inn. Maybe I should go back and get them, you think. But right now, you're here, in front of the curio shop, and you may as well investigate this place on your own.

You shove their image out of your mind and slowly push open the door.

The door opens smoothly, and a small bell at the top of the door rings sweetly. In the back, you see a small shadow move against the wall, and a thin, ancient voice pipes up, "Eh? Who's there?"

You stand surrounded by the still, dusty shapes of statues and candelabra, by artwork and tapestries and strange and wonderful artifacts from across the world. Your nose is filled with the musty scent of age and antiquity, of dust from the distant past, and you absently reach out to admire a long, decorative spear from some far-off land.

The shadow in the back comes around an aisle of curios, and a small, old man enters into view, his candle casting a soft orange glow on his wrinkled features. He blinks at you from behind a thick pair of spectacles. "And who might you be, young sir, visiting my shop at an hour when all others are asleep?"

"Asleep?" you say. "My name is Shadow. My friends and I are . . . exploring," you tell him, for you do not wish to reveal your mision against Lord Fear. "We came to Arnstadt to find rooms for the night; but there is no one asleep here in the village, no one at all, save for my friends. The town, except for you, sir, has been abandoned."

The old man scoffs at you. "Tut-tut. No, no, it is simply very late, my boy. You don't know how rural the villagers of Arnstadt really are. The streets here roll up shortly after sundown, and—"

You shake your head and interrupt him. "I only wish that were so. Your candlelight is the only sign of someone alive that we have found. Something terrible has happened here. The villagers are gone, and somehow you are the only one left."

The old man looks into your eyes, then turns away. "Gone? Then it is Lord Fear," he says, muttering. "It has to be! The monster has stolen them for some nefarious purpose of his . . ."

He sighs and starts toward the back. "Follow me, boy. I suppose we must talk."

The old man leads you around shelves of artifacts to a small office, hidden behind dusty layers of books and

DUNGEON OF FEAR

papers and a few odd, assorted pieces of pottery. You are struck by two impressive objects sitting on his desk: a crystal globe, situated in a tripod of gold and silver, and an ornate, mechanical timepiece made out of gold. It is ticking softly.

"It is Lord Fear," the old man says again. "He is behind this, I'm sure of it. I left the village a few days ago on a buying trip beyond the forest and returned only a few minutes ago. I suppose that is why I was spared from the same fate as the rest of the village."

Your eyes are captivated by the way the light shines and flickers in the depths of his mysterious crystal ball, and plays wondrously along the curved gold of the timepiece. Perhaps your infatuation with the items is why you do not notice that if the old man has just returned from somewhere, you can see no bed roll or baggage anywhere in the shop.

The old man smiles at you. "Ah, they caught your eye, did they? And well they should. These beauties are rarities from the east. A crystal globe, capable, wizards say, of showing scenes of the past, present, or future. And this," he says, gesturing, "a mechanical timepiece of untold age and design. It has never stopped working in over one thousand years, the legends say, and was created by a race forgotten in the mists of time. Do you like them, boy?"

You cannot help but grin. The light shining off them is so beautiful, and you cannot take your eyes off them. They are captivating your every thought.

You hear the old man's voice as though through a muffled haze. "Tell you what, boy. Pick one. Pick one, the one you like better, and it's yours."

It is too late for you, but you are too mesmerized to know just how trapped you are. Your entire world is nothing but the gleam of wondrous light playing off the timepiece and the crystal ball. And the old man wants to give you one! You! A treasure like this! What a nice man he is! One of these trasures will be yours!

Is yours!

If you choose the globe, go to 69.

If you choose the clock, go to 54.

64

Going off in search of your friend's wizard might help you find the thief of the crystal skull. But you think back to the scene in the king's vault, and in your heart you believe that tracking down the wizard will just take up too much time.

"I think the clues in the vault were clear," you say. Dare looks at you as though he has found a new ally. "We are dealing with the undead, for who else could have left those footprints, distinct with bones? And the cleric said he had detected the aura of unnatural evil. No, I think we should proceed to the lair of Lord Fear as quickly as possible and find the crystal skull long before the cleric's spell will bring us back."

Dare grunts in approval. Keela nods and says, "Very well. I doubt the mage could have done anything good for us anyway. I've heard rumors from others that he is no longer to be trusted. He may now be allied with darkness."

"By all means, then, we should avoid him," you say. "Dealing with Lord Fear will be more than enough darkness for me."

The three of you begin again on your journey along the forest road, heading north toward the Forest of Shades and Lord Fear's ancestral estate, Carnivex Mansion. The ride through the forest is warm and pleasant, and the songs of the birds and the way the light filters through the trees leaves you with a peaceful, hypnotic feeling, a feeling that nothing can go wrong.

You hope.

A few hours later, you stop for rest and a meal in a wide clearing along the forest road. On one side of the road, you leave your horses to be tended at a small stable; then you cross the dirt path and enter an inn dominating the other side. Talbot, the happy, heavyset proprietor of the Green Hole Tavern (so named for the natural clearing in the wood), seats you himself and brings over bowls of stew and thick, fresh bread. He asks for news of the realm, as you're his first visitors today, but you tell him nothing of your quest. Even this friendly fellow could owe allegiance to Lord Fear, and he could send word ahead that you are coming. Instead you exchange such news that would not arouse suspicion, and when you're finished, the three of you set off again for the north.

The warmth of the afternoon sun, even under the shadowy branches of the forest, makes you perspire lightly. The trek is fairly easy to make over land, as the ground is flat until the last leg of the journey, where the border into the north is marked with a line of round hills. You estimate that you should reach Lord Fear's estate about an hour or more before sundown, and that should give you a little time to search the grounds for the crystal skull and get out by nightfall, for Lord Fear's powers increase when the sun is down.

To make the ride seem shorter, Keela again tells you the story of her previous battle against Lord Fear and the eventual defeat of Teraptus, the evil mage. The warrior interrupts frequently, embellishing the story to make it appear that his prowess and strength contributed more to Teraptus's downfall than the cooperation between the four fighters and the friend they found in Teraptus's castle, a dwarf with a mystical hammer.

You are proud of Keela's involvement in the defeat of Teraptus, for you had long known that the wizard's villainy was growing across the land. You don't know quite what to make of the defeat, though, for it seems to you that evil rarely dies. Yes, Teraptus lost the battle, but was he vanquished forever, as you hope, or did he simply transport himself away, to build his strength until he was ready to return and again battle the forces of good?

A cold chill travels up your spine. You hope that the evil of Teraptus is gone, but something inside you says that the wizard will make a return sooner or later—and you hope it's much later.

Dare surprises you late in the afternoon. Your group has traveled a long distance without speaking, and suddenly Dare breaks out in song, his voice echoing through the trees. His songs are ballads and tales of battle, of war stories and legends of bravery and valor. Despite Dare's brawny appearance and single-minded quest for action, he sings beautifully and in a clear, strong voice, and you can well imagine tales of his own bravery being sung on quests and around campfires ages into the future.

Dare sings his songs of glory long into the afternoon. You allow him and Keela to ride a little ahead, for you still don't want them to know about your newest find, the pouch from the vault.

Their horses make a slow turn along the path through the forest, and you remove the pouch from your pocket and examine it.

Its red velvet exterior is soft and smooth, and the pouch shows no sign of age. The drawstring is made of golden string—no, you realize, real gold, spun delicately in the elven fashion and twisted into a decorative rope. You whistle softly at your valuable find, then turn the pouch over. On the other side, elven letters of gold and silver have been woven into the velvet. You recognize the words as an ancient language of the elves—High Elvish, you think they call it—and, though you cannot read any language but your own, you think that one word is somewhat familiar—*illysari*—and you're pretty sure it is the elven word for "infinity."

You squeeze the sides of the pouch, but you cannot tell if there is anything inside it or not. You carefully untie the drawstring, keeping an eye on your companions ahead. They still aren't paying you much attention, so you slowly pull open the mouth of the pouch and look inside.

The pouch is empty, lined with dull black that reflects

very little light. It seems odd for such a fancy piece of craftsmanship as the outside of the pouch. You shrug. Ah, well. It would have been great if there had been gold or jewels inside, but at least you've got a nice pouch now to hold things.

The forest begins to thin out, and soon you and your companions find yourselves at the crest of a hill. Below you stretches a hilly plain that signifies the border into the northern part of the realm, and there, in the distance, at the edge of the Forest of Shades, you see a squat, dark house, standing like a lone sentinel with eyes of darkness.

"Carnivex Mansion," the warrior says. He looks up at the sun. "If we hurry, we'll have about an hour to explore the house before the sun sets."

"I don't want to stay longer than that," the thief says, adjusting the short sword at her hip. "Who knows what foul things Lord Fear has conjured up in there?"

"All right," you say. "Let's go."

The three of you urge your horses down the hill toward the mansion and ride forth at a brisk gallop. You think Dare was a bit optimistic; the sun is lower than he thought, and you might have thirty or forty-five minutes in the mansion at the most. Well, you think, warriors are not valued for their mental prowess, but for their skills with swords and clubs.

The house seems to loom ever closer, and soon you find yourselves at a cast iron gate set into a stone fence surrounding the Carnivex estate. The black gate hangs twisted from the stonework as though some violent explosion had torn it from its hinges, and the mansion beyond seems to watch you malevolently, its windows black and empty, like the eyes of the dead.

You don't like it here. There's no reason you should, considering the evil incarnate that is Lord Fear. But the house seems to be watching you, as though it knows you're here. It is filled with darkness, and already your skin feels cold just thinking about going inside for some crystal skull that you had nothing to do with.

You are a long way off from the seat of the realm, with only Keela and a simple warrior as companions. Idly, you think that maybe the cleric's spell is not very powerful. The cleric himself was visibly weakened when he cast the spell of protection in the vault; perhaps the spell to transport you back has been weakened as well.

Dare rides through the open gate, and the thief follows. She looks back and shouts, "Shadow, come on! We've haven't much time before sundown!"

Your horse whinnies and steps backward, mirroring the hesitation you feel. This is your chance to escape. You consider your options: Lord Fear inside the mansion, or a fifty-fifty chance of escape out here in the wilderness, where no one will ever find you.

What do you do?

If you go through the gate with your companions, go to 30.

If you try to escape, go to 55.

65

The sword or the skull? Of course, the sword is your weapon of choice, and you know you could reach it in time. But the skull has powers that are unknown, and perhaps it could hurt Lord Fear where plain metal would fail.

You leap without thinking. You lash out with a foot and kick Lord Fear's hand away. Then you tumble to the ground and leap up onto the king's dais, the skull and staff in your hands.

It gleams in the torchlight, and you feel it throbbing in your hands, vibrating with power.

Lord Fear howls in rage and storms you.

You shout "No!" at the black mage, and you feel the power locked with the skull and staff surge through you, as though you are a funnel, a living conduit of energy.

The skull's eyes gleam with arcane fires, and a lancing beam of golden energy slices through the undead warriors and drops them to the floor, sending Lord Fear's death knights to their true deaths.

The fire burns through you. You now understand some of the words the cleric quoted to you. The skull and staff have some power over undeath, whether to create the undead, or destroy them, or return them to life. Lord Fear screams again, taking a fearful step backward. Another flank of death knights approaches you, and with a shout you aim a bolt of radiant energy directly into their midst, blasting away their decomposed bones and flesh and letting their souls find true peace.

Lord Fear's concentration visibly lessens. He backs away from you in terror, and his undead servants shamble about aimlessly, without direction.

You step off the dais and approach him. He mutters words in an ancient tongue. Circles of black power glow around his clawlike hands, and you realize he is casting a spell of darkness to protect himself.

The skull instantly reacts to your knowledge, and a burst of golden energy blasts out of the skull's eyes and blows Lord Fear into the wall.

His zombies collapse to the floor as he loses his power over them. He stands and refocuses at you, and you can feel the dark energies building up around him.

The anger and hatred at this foul beast well up inside you. They churn through you like liquid fire, making you strong, focusing the skull's innate powers.

Fear's eyes roll back as he casts his spell.

You feel utter calm wash over you like a cool breeze. Then a lightning bolt of pure energy lances from the skull and engulfs the dark lord. He screams as it burns away the layers of evil and hatred.

Again the skull flares out with a bolt of power, and Lord Fear is swallowed in a fireball of light and energy. He screams as the purifying fires eat away at his evil.

His shrieks echo through the hall. Then the power from the skull subsides, and you fall to your knees.

Keela helps you to your feet, and together you walk over to Lord Fear.

The warrior points. "I don't understand," he says.

The smoke from where Lord Fear burned rises from the floor. But Lord Fear is gone. All that is left, all that has been distilled and transmogrified by the power of the Crystal Skull of Sa'arkloth, is a single black jewel, larger than all the rubies in your pouch, a gem encasing the corrupted life-force of Lord Fear.

You pick up the ebony gem and place it in a deep pocket, where he—it—can do no harm. Then, together, the three of you stride victorious out of the castle of Fear, and into the cool, crisp night.

Go to 31.

66

Dawn, you wonder, what is it about the dawn . . . ?

You smack your forehead with the palm of your hand.

"What is it?" Keela asks as she jumps upon her horse.

"The clues! The ghosts' clues! How could I have been so stupid?"

You shake your head and lean angrily against your horse.

"The cleric told us, back in the palace. Remember that legend? The skull has the power—what did he say?—over undeath and rebirth." You open your arms and twirl in the street. "Lord Fear came through here with the skull! He did something with it, used its power to transform the villagers into something else. Look around you," you cry. "The villagers haven't gone anywhere. The villagers are these trees!"

Keela and Dare approach you, then together you examine one of the trees up close. This close, the tree appears less like a tree of the forest, and more like something made to resemble a tree, shapeshifted into this form through pain and suffering, against its will.

"How did you know this?" Dare says.

"The other clue. 'The scarlet prisoners can be freed in the risen light.' " You point to the sun, rising above the trees to the east. "Dawn, the rising sun. And the scarlet prisoners must be those gems back in the castle vault." You smack yourself again. "I should have known it when I felt the gems humming in my hand. Fear must have used the power of the skull to steal the villagers' life-forces away, in the same way the skull transformed Fear into the black gem."

"But Fear wasn't turned into a tree," Keela says.

"Lord Fear was not really alive, like the villagers. He embraced undeath long ago. The skull transformed his body into what it truly was: nothingness. Evil.

"Fear himself must have changed the villagers into the form of a tree, perhaps as some kind of twisted joke."

"We must return to the castle and get the gems," Dare says.

You shrug. "It won't do any good until dawn tomorrow. And we cannot stay that long. The cleric's spell will return us to the realm later today."

"I suggest we ride," Keela says. "The gems will still be here in a few days, and the mages of King Halvor can return here and restore the village to life properly."

You feel a smile of contentment form across your face. "Now, that's a good idea. Come on, warrior. Let's go home, and leave the magic to magic-users."

Dare grunts his assent. "I am all for that. Let us return to the realm!"

Go to 70.

67

You look toward the dimness inside the conservatory and shudder involuntarily. Since the mansion was abandoned, many of the stronger plants have crept up the glass wall and spread across the conservatory like a grotesque spiderweb. A feeling falls over you like a cold shadow; you do not want to go in there. The plants just don't seem . . . right to you somehow.

But you briefly examine the marble fireplace, and there doesn't seem to be anything here for you. You look back toward the conservatory. It is large—large enough to hide a dozen crystal skulls—and you know instinctively that the chances are much higher that the skull lies hidden in there.

Dare opens the glass door of the conservatory, and the green, sweet odor of decomposing plants and stale earth washes over you like a shroud.

The three of you enter the conservatory and instantly break into a sweat. The temperature in here is at least ten degrees higher, and you are overwhelmed by the moistness of the surrounding plants.

The three of you split up. The thief and warrior take the aisles to the left and right, and you search through the center aisle leading to the far, rear wall. You take out your short sword and use the tip to search through dirt in planters and pots, to spread apart the leaves of dying bushes and plants that are weakly reaching up toward the distant sun. Most of the plants are dead or dying from many months of inattention, but several are quite hearty, surviving—or even thriving—off the moist heat and soil that is rich with decomposing plants. One plant in particular, a long, thick vine sprouting green leaves and short, sharp thorns, seems to have taken over the conservatory and stretches from wall to wall, even growing up the sides of the greenhouse and across the glass ceiling in a huge green web.

Or a net, you think suspiciously.

Without warning, a startling image comes to your mind: the vine above you, dropping from the ceiling, enveloping you and your companions in a living web. It's a trap, you think unconsciously. This whole room is a trap!

You open your mouth to shout a warning . . . but you never get a chance to yell, for in the aisle to the left, Keela suddenly screams with terror. You turn, and you discover a part of the long, leafy vine twined around Keela like a snake coiling around its prey.

You slice your way through the barrier of plants and leap into the left aisle. Dare crashes through the plants behind you, and together you raise your swords to save Keela. But the warrior's feet are suddenly pulled out from under him, and he falls to the ground, a vine wrapping around his legs and creeping toward his neck. The thorns prick his skin and bring blood to the air, and the plant seems to taste it, then absorb it through its leaves, as though it is feeding.

You take a step toward your companions. Then a shadow falls over you from above, and the image that came to your mind suddenly becomes real. The plant falls upon you like a living, twisting net and tightens over you until it is hard for you to breathe. The sword falls from your useless hand, and you feel a thorn pierce your skin and lap your precious lifeblood.

You try to squirm away, but a creeper bends down from the ceiling. It is the bulbous head of the blood-drinking plant, and it slowly descends, almost as though it is sniffing the air, and finally sniffs its way down your head and to the hollow of your neck.

You feel a cold, searing pain as something pierces your flesh. Within seconds, you cannot move, and your body burns inside with an icefire that is colder than the winter snows. The vine does the same to your companions, and soon they are paralyzed like you.

You have a lot of time to think about your fate, for your transformation is a slow one. The plant is evil, a growth from a plane or universe far beyond your mortal existence.

Transplanted here by some mage or wizard—probably Lord Fear during an early experiment with the powers of darkness—the plant feeds on terror and human blood. And it reproduces with its bite, which slowly transforms its prey into a living version of itself.

* * * * *

In time, you can move. With your newfound senses of smell and an inexplicable way to sense patterns of light and movement, you examine yourself. You're proud of the leafy tendrils that used to be your arms and legs, and your podlike head can stretch almost to the ceiling.

In time, you will grow. And perhaps your master, Lord Fear, will someday return to feed you with the blood of his enemies—the humans you once called your brethren.

Until that day, you will grow . . . and wait . . .

The End

68

The cleric's spell has suddenly returned you to the palace of King Halvor. The three of you face the king together, and Dare recounts your entire journey to the king's assemblage. No aspect of your adventure is left untouched, and Dare deliberately embellishes your brave actions and impresses the king with your valiant attempts to recover the crystal skull. Dare must have grown fond of you. Inwardly, you smile. He is all right, for a warrior.

Finally, King Halvor rises from his throne and considers what course of action he must take. Lord Fear has conquered the village of Arnstadt. The monster still possesses the crystal skull, and his actions indicate that he intends to conquer the entire realm with his legions of the undead.

The king turns to you, a look of determination on his usually scowling face. "For the service to your king and to the realm—and despite the failure to return the skull to me—I hereby grant you your freedom."

You are amazed at the king's generosity. Keela smiles broadly at you, as though she is thinking, "We've gotten ourselves out of this problem!"

"Except for you, Shadow," the king says, "until you have returned the Emerald Collar of the Lady Carnassia."

His Red Dragons surround you. You swallow nervously, then decide to finally give up. The collar is obviously too important; you would never be able to fence it now.

Besides, with your freedom, you can always steal back the collar when the opportunity arises.

"I never had the collar, Your Majesty," you admit, smiling. "It has been hidden in your own palace all this time. Shall I retrieve it for you?"

The king's face turns an angry red, then he bursts out in laughter. "All this time," he says, chuckling. "That's almost as good as what you did with Bleehall's gold tooth."

With an escort of guards, you march to the hall where you hid the collar and reach down behind a long mahogany armoire. You pluck out a hidden pouch, and present it to the king in his audience chamber.

The king takes out the emerald collar, glowing deep inside with fires of jade. He nods, approving. "Thank you for your services, Shadow. For a common thief, you have proved yourself highly trustworthy. Until I need you again . . . don't let me see you around here. Guards!"

The guards escort you and Keela to the castle doors. Together you go out into the sunlight, where your friends from the bazaar surround you and greet you happily.

But something inside you knows that, despite your newfound freedom, your quest was not completely successful. The village of Arnstadt is still mysteriously abandoned, and you did nothing to hinder the evil schemes of Lord Fear.

You shrug, swallowing your apprehensions. The day is bright and sunny, and you have many friends around

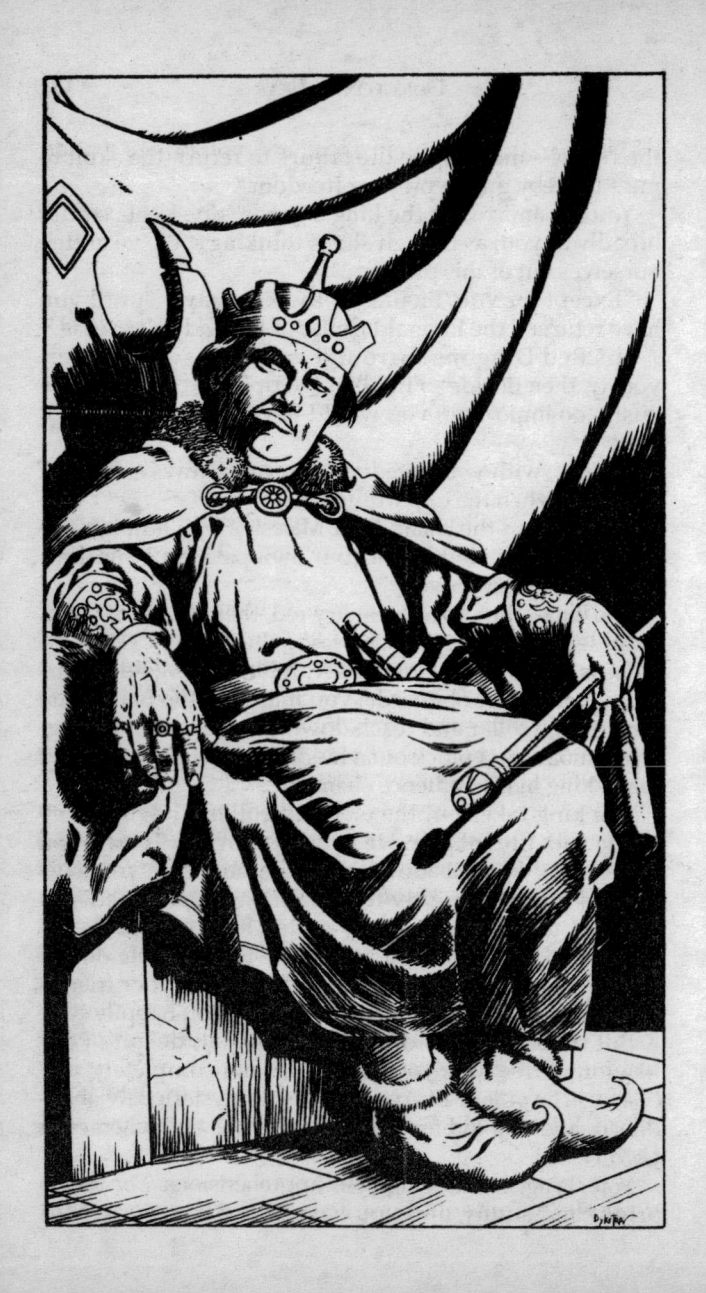

you. Long days of freedom await, and you cannot wait to begin your next adventure.

The End

69

As you stare at the artifacts on the desk, the old man's words echo in your mind: "Pick one, the one you like better, and it's yours."

Your eyes flick back and forth between the crystal ball and the wondrous clock. Slowly, you reach out, first toward one, then toward the other. Without thinking, you make your decision . . . and your hand closes on the crystal ball.

Instantly, your eyes are filled with ethereal, shimmering light, flowing into you almost as though from the secret depths of the crystal itself. The crystal grows warm in your hand, and its warmth spreads like numbness throughout your body, filling you with serenity.

As if from a great distance, you hear the old man's voice say, "Did you really think that anyone could escape from the hunger of Lord Fear? Now, Arnstadt is his to do with as he pleases, and you and your friends stand no chance against his magical might! They will be captured and turned into his undead slaves just as easily as you!"

But the old man's words fade to a whisper. You float in light, silently, soundlessly, a captive within the heart of Lord Fear's crystal trap. If you could think, you would realize that the curio shop had been a trap for travelers and wayfarers. Now that you are caught, your friends at the inn will soon be dealt with.

But you cannot care about friendship or the fate of the realm. It feels just too calm, too good, to care about anything.

It is timeless and peaceful in the crystal globe that is your eternal prison. Lord Fear will soon overrun the world with his evil powers, but you cannot care.

Your world is all brilliance and warmth and light.

And if you could think, you would know that, now, you are nothing. Nothing but a glimmer, a spark, flickering in a serene sea of undulating light, caught in the depths of a beautiful crystal ball . . .

Forever . . .

The End

70

Your quest to find the crystal skull is over, and your journey from the village of Arnstadt is peaceful and uneventful.

Your return to the realm is quite different. Scouts who had been watching for you raced ahead and informed the king. It is after nightfall when the three of you finally ride up through the castle gates and stop before the keep. The moon is high and bright in the crystal-clear sky, casting its silver rays on you with a brilliance and clarity you have not seen in a long time—perhaps because the darkness of Lord Fear has been dispelled.

You dismount before the keep, and the king's Red Dragons greet you as if you are royalty. They hold open the keep's doors and escort you directly to the king's chambers.

King Halvor stands at your approach. "The fellowship is returned!" he announces. "Was the quest successful?"

You drop to one knee and bow your head. "Your Majesty, we have journeyed far and fought hard. In the village of Arnstadt, we discovered the foul mage who had stolen the crystal skull, and we defeated him in combat.

"We bring you gifts, Your Majesty, souvenirs of our journey to the dungeon of Lord Fear."

You take the pouch from your belt and untie the golden drawstring. "Your Highness," you say, reaching in, "I present to you ... Lord Fear."

The king gasps. You remove your hand from the pouch and hold the black gem up between your fingers. It hums against your flesh, pulsating with evil life. "Lord Fear, Your Majesty—that is, all that is left of him."

Suddenly, you get an idea. The moon is clearly visible through the tall windows set in the walls. Perhaps, if you hold up the gem so that the moonlight streams through it, the king will get a much more impressive image of the gem's power.

You take a step toward the king and hold out the gem.

If you hold the gem up to the moonlight, go to 35.

If you give the gem to the king, go to 74.

71

You shrug. It is a toss up, isn't it? The dream you had really told you nothing. The lion or the bird?

"Go ahead," you tell Dare. "Lets see what happens."

The warrior tugs on the bird's ring, but the iron device is bolted securely into the stone of the crypt. He pulls again and grunts with the effort, but tugging the bird's ring gives no result.

He lets go of the iron ring and claps rust off his hand. "Now what?" he says.

If you pull the lion's ring, go to 11.

If you decide to return to the Red Room Inn, go to 46.

72

The doors to the keep slam shut behind you. You're in a wide entrance chamber, hung with finely woven tapestries depicting the history of the realm. Torches cast their warm glow on you, but the guard behind you shoves you forward, toward another set of doors, and you have no time to examine the castle's obvious wealth.

The guards lead you through a maze of corridors, only some of which you remember from your rapid flight through the castle months ago. Then you turn a corner, and you spy a very familiar mahogany armoire. You forced yourself months ago to memorize the long cabinet and the tapestry hanging behind it, a lush landscape woven with gold and silver strands. It was here that you hid for a few brief seconds when the guards were chasing you through the keep, and you can't believe your luck in finding it again so soon. If only they knew . . .

You proceed through the castle, then are held at the wide doors to the king's audience chamber. Your guard announces your names to the Red Dragons posted at the door, and the word is passed into the chamber.

The doors swing open silently, and the guards shove you and Keela forward. Your footsteps echo through the huge room, and you look around you with amazement at the tall, carved marble columns, the golden statues positioned in the corners, the decorative flags and standards and tapestries draped from the ceiling and along the walls. If this is what the audience chamber is like, you can just imagine the gold and wealth hoarded in the treasury. . . .

The guards bring you to a halt only a few yards from a marble dais, upon which is positioned a throne made of gold and silver and ornately decorated with rare, dazzling jewels. The king sits there watching you, frowning, his golden crown glinting atop his head. Beside him proudly stand the king's cleric and a tall warrior in a silver and purple cloak, who resembles a powerful lion with his long, flowing mane of hair. The king's imperious vizier approaches from the other side and tells the king, "Thieves, Your Majesty—"

"Yes, I can see that," the king snaps. The vizier takes a step back. The guards force you both to your knees.

The king looks at Keela, then at you. He points at Keela. "Despite your assistance to the crown in the matter of the wizard Teraptus, you are charged with the crime of breaking into the royal treasury and stealing the Crystal Skull of Sa'arkloth. How do you plead?"

She throws back her hair defiantly. "I have stolen nothing from the treasury, Your Highness," she says. "I have not been inside the keep since the night our fellowship returned from the castle of Teraptus and I personally gave you the jewels that we found there."

He looks at her coldly. "How do you plead?"

She draws herself up. "I am innocent, Your Majesty."

He turns. "And you," he says. He turns to the guards. "Why is this one here?" he says, pointing at you.

"Your Majesty," says the vizier, grinning, "this is the criminal known as Shadow."

The king gapes at you, then snaps his mouth shut and drums his fingers on the edge of the throne. "Shadow," he says softly. "This is a surprise. So you have returned to the scene of the crime."

"Your Highness," you begin, but you are cut off as the king leaps to his feet and shouts, "Silence!"

His voice rings throughout the chamber. The king asks, "Were they discovered together?"

"Aye, Your Majesty," your guard answers. "Conspiring to commit another crime against the realm, most likely, in the Rose and Crown, a notorious thieves' den, Sire."

The king sits again in the throne and watches you. After a long silence, he slowly says, "And what have you done with the Emerald Collar of the Lady Carnassia?"

You shake your head. "My lord, I have nothing to do with it. I am innocent—"

"Please, please, please," the king says. "Do not try my intelligence. We saw you, thief, right in this very chamber.

You ripped the emerald collar right off the Lady Carnassia's throat. The only way you have of avoiding a horrifying doom is to tell me where you are keeping the collar."

"Your Majesty," you say, "it is common knowledge in the realm that I am of the Guild of Thieves. However, the emerald collar is not mine. I do not have it. Do not ask me to admit something that I cannot."

The king shifts in his throne, the fires of anger smoldering in his eyes. Finally, he announces, "Shadow, you are charged with the theft of the Emerald Collar of the Lady Carnassia, and with conspiring with Keela here in the theft of the Crystal Skull of Sa'arkloth. If you are found guilty, your sentence will be life imprisonment in the royal dungeons. How do you plead?"

Life imprisonment! Well, you certainly can't admit to anything about the emerald collar without having a legal advisor present. And concerning this skull, you know absolutely nothing. You cannot help the king recover his treasure at all. Guilty or not, it looks like you'll be seeing the inside of the king's dungeons for a long time.

"Your Majesty," you say, "I have had nothing to do with the burglary of the royal treasury. I have just returned to the realm after a long absence, and I met my friend in the Rose and Crown for a drink. Neither of us had anything to do with the theft of any skull. Your Highness, I am not guilty."

The king sighs. He stares at you in stony silence. Then he stands, and his voice echoes through the chamber like peals of thunder. "Very well. In the absence of advisors or contradictory evidence from the accused, I hereby find you both guilty of crimes against the crown, and I sentence you to—"

"Wait!" you cry out, rising to your feet. The guards surround you for fear you will attack the king, but you are too busy thinking to bother with physical threats. Perhaps there is a way to get you and Keela out of this, without seeing the insides of the dungeons ever again.

"My lord," you say, "incarceration in the dungeons will punish us for crimes we did not commit. It will serve no purpose except to please the crown. However, I believe there is a way we can both be satisfied."

You don't even give the king time to respond. "My liege, give us a chance to prove our innocence. If you want proof, allow us to go free for one week, just enough time for us to discover the true thief of the treasury. Give us a chance to return the Crystal Skull of Sa'arkloth to you, its rightful owner."

The king watches you, then abruptly laughs. "Let you go free? Hah! That's a good one!" He returns to his throne. "And give you a chance to escape with both the collar and the crystal skull? Do you take me for a fool?"

Wisely, you do not answer him. Instead, you lead him on. "Your Majesty, let us assume that we are innocent. This will give us a chance to prove that. Who better to track down a thief than another thief? Better yet, two thieves. We can have your skull back in your hands before you realize we're even gone."

You approach the dais. "If we are guilty, yes, we could escape. But what if you had your cleric place an enchantment on us—a spell that would transport us back to this spot if we attempted to escape, and would also return us here at the exact moment that one week was up? You will have your treasure—if we can find it—and if we can't, you will still have us as your prisoners."

The king rubs his chin in thought. You've got him! "And if you succeed, thief? What do you propose then?"

You look down at your feet, as though you are pleading for mercy. "If we are successful in our quest, my lord, I ask that we be given our freedom, for it will then be proven that we are not the thieves you want. If we do not return the skull to you, you may do with us as you please. My only request is that you give us the opportunity to prove our loyalty to the crown."

The royal vizier wrings his hands in frustration. "My lord, certainly you cannot believe the words of a mere thief—"

"Be quiet, vizier!" the king says. He fixes you with his

gaze and taps his fingers. "Cleric!" he calls. "Is a spell such as the thief described possible?"

The cleric steps forward to stand beside the king. A glance passes between the cleric and Keela, and you think you see him smile slightly at her. The cleric replies, "Indeed, Your Highness. A spell of this nature is more complex, more taxing, than simpler spells, but it can be cast with ease." He clears his throat. "And, if I might add, my liege, the female thief has aided the crown before, and my powers can detect no deception with her or Shadow in the matter of the skull. This quest of theirs might prove just the thing to return to us the crystal skull, without sending half the royal guardsmen to the far corners of the realm in search of it."

The king nods slowly in thought, then stands. "So be it!" he says. "Cleric, prepare to cast your spell. I accept your offer, thieves. But a week will afford you far too many opportunities to escape my cleric's wizardry. You have exactly two days from this point—no more—to return the skull to me. Two days. And if you reappear before me without the crystal skull, then I know that, either by treachery or failure, you will have stolen the skull for your own purposes, or have been unable to find it in the realm.

"It is no matter, for without the skull you will be locked inside the lower dungeons with only rabid vermin for friends, and you will never be free to walk the realm again. And if you try to escape, your sentence shall be . . . death."

You and Keela can only nod at the king's harsh words. To him, you are nothing more than common criminals, and the concept of being innocent until proven guilty has no meaning to the one person who makes all the laws of the land. You now have to prove yourself to your king and the realm. At least you have a chance to demonstrate your innocence and stay free.

"There shall be no attempt to escape, my lord," you say, glancing at Keela. She nods at you. "Your judgment is right and good, and we are honored by the chance to prove our innocence to the realm. When shall we begin?"

The king motions with his hand, and the cleric approaches you. Then the king tells his warrior to stand with you.

The cleric raises his hands high. His eyes roll back, showing only the whites.

The cleric's voice is neither soft nor loud, but it echoes through the hall with a power all its own. You feel the room become stuffy, as though the air inside is tightening, like a ball. "On the winds of the moon and stars . . . I summon the energies of the Chariot of Night! Let these travelers find their way home, not by their desire, but by my command!" Flickers of blue fire, like lightning born out of some strange landscape, play along the chamber's ceiling, swirling like a galaxy. "I call you! Cl'yhthnotep! Mermus! Hystaliis! All the breaths of the winds of the sea and land, in the earth and above! Return these wanderers two suns from this moment . . . or when one flees from his appointed path! I summon you! Hear my words and obey!"

At that moment, the blue lights dancing on the ceiling flare brilliantly, diving down to absorb you. Your skin tingles both hot and cold as the energies summoned by the cleric seep through your pores and burn inside you with a cold fire. You scream aloud as the blue light burns into your bones, and you watch as your skeleton glows brightly inside your flesh—

Then you find yourself facedown on the floor, where you have fallen. You shake your head groggily. Guards help you to your feet, and you once again face the royal dais.

"The spell has taken," the cleric says, standing beside the king. "The thieves are ready to begin their quest. There will be no escape."

The king raises his voice. "Now, thieves, you must find the Crystal Skull of Sa'arkloth. You are free to go wherever you wish, but you must return here with the crystal skull in two days' time . . . or face imprisonment." He gestures, and the bronzed warrior steps over to the female thief.

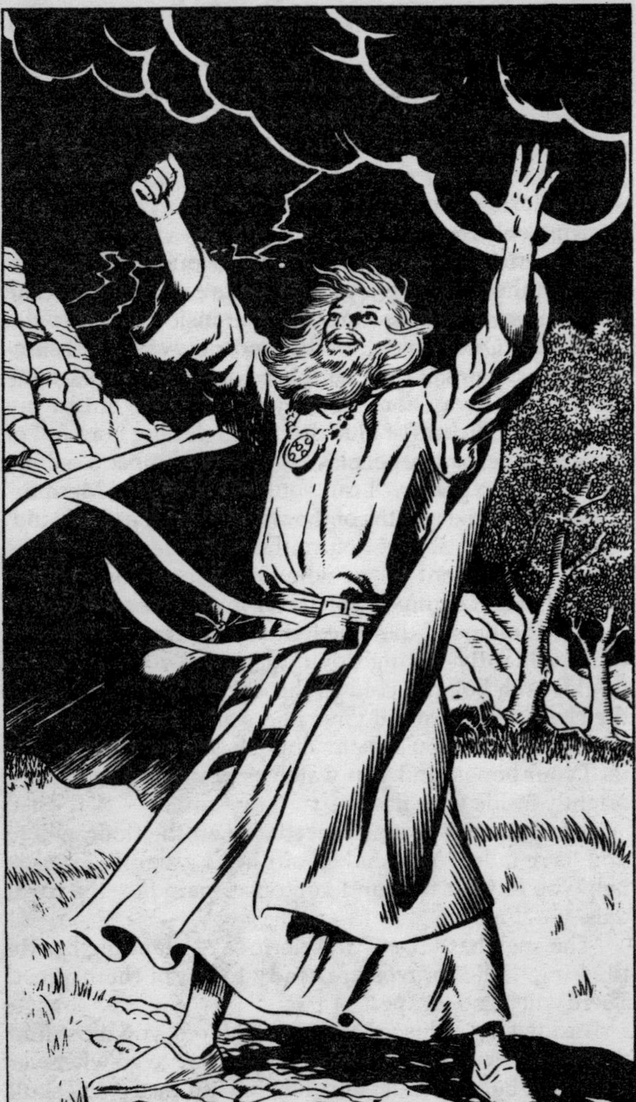

Keela nods at him, and you see that they know each other. "One of my most valiant warriors, Dare, shall accompany you on your quest, to protect you in times of trouble and to ensure the safety of the skull. Now, where do you wish to begin?"

You think for a moment. If a thief had stolen the skull, he probably would have tried to sell it to a black marketeer—"fence"—of the realm. And you probably know more fences than anyone else in the castle.

But you know nothing of the thief or how he broke into the treasury. Perhaps you should request to visit the vault and examine the scene of the crime.

If you want to examine the vault, go to 57.

If you want to speak with a marketeer, go to 8.

73

Your decision comes quickly, impulsively. You look back to your friends, then step out into the village street.

The shop is just a short walk across the square. Your footsteps are the only sounds you hear, and a wave of loneliness washes over you. You fleetingly consider turning back for the safety and warmth of the inn, but your mind is made up.

The shop window is filled with antiques and artifacts from ages gone by, from kingdoms you can only dream about. The sign in the window reads simply

ARNSTADT CURIOS
M. Speller, Proprietor

You gaze through the window. There, far in the back and hidden by row upon row of old curiosities, you spy the warm glow of a candle flickering among the shadows.

You twist the doorknob. The door is unlocked.

For an instant, you debate the wisdom of your choice. You cannot deny that you want to find out who is inside this shop, but you also cannot deny that coming here without your friends is not the wisest decision you have ever made.

You yawn. Maybe you are getting tired now. You still have time to change your mind.

If you go inside the curio shop, go to 63.

If you return to the Red Room Inn, go to 21.

74

At the last minute, you decide to simply give the black gem to the king. You never know what kind of wizardry might occur under cover of darkness, and the light of the moon might just be some secret trigger that would unleash a horror that you cannot even imagine upon the realm.

At least, you don't want to take that chance.

You approach the king, the black gem in your hand. At a gesture from King Halvor, his cleric takes the obsidian gem and clutches it tightly in his hand. If you read the king's cleric right, Lord Fear will never be restored to life, and the gem will be locked forever behind the doors of the tightest, most secret vault the cleric can find.

You hold up the pouch. "Your Majesty, I present to you this pouch of wonders, which I . . . discovered . . . on our travels."

The cleric looks at you oddly, then allows himself a secret smile. He knows exactly where you found that pouch, and he is visibly proud that you are returning it.

"And what is so wondrous about a mere pouch?" the king asks.

You reach inside again. "Witness, my lord, our third and final gift." And you slowly pull out the completed Staff of Sa'arkloth, impossibly long for a pouch that small.

The skull gleams with light and power, and you humbly lay it at your king's feet. "My lord, the skull is returned to you, restored for the first time in hundreds of years. These things we bring you, with news of the fall of Fear."

The cleric hustles the prizes away to the royal vault, and the three of you relate the story of your journey to the king.

When you are finished with your incredible tale of the village of Arnstadt, King Halvor rises and places his hand upon your shoulder. "I was wrong about you, Shadow. I thought you nothing more than a common thief. In reality, the heroics of you and your friends may have saved the realm."

He draws himself up. "I hereby decree that, due to your actions against an enemy of the realm and your extraordinary service to your king, you are free to go!" He smiles. "Go now, thieves. The horses that brought you back are yours to keep. Go in peace, and know that you have the eternal thanks of your king."

You bow in honor to King Halvor, and you and Keela leave the king's chamber.

You cannot believe that you came out of this alive, much less a hero. And you will have a great story to tell your friends back at the Rose and Crown.

You laugh and grab Keela by the arm, whispering, "Come on."

Unescorted by the king's guards, you lead Keela through the halls of the castle until you come to an alcove where a long mahogany armoire is situated. You casually glance around for onlookers, then, spying no one, you reach behind the armoire and pluck out a large leather pouch. You stuff it in your tunic and hurry away.

"What is that?" Keela asks.

"Outside. You'll see."

Outside, the two horses, gifts from the king, await you. You ride them quickly through the gates, then slow down to a trot on the road leading to Keela's home village.

You take the pouch out of your tunic and open it for her. Moonlight gleams like jade fire inside the large emerald and glints with starlight off the polished gold.

"The emerald collar!" Keela says.

You laugh. "I never had it. I hid it right under the king's nose the night it was stolen. Now . . ." You pause. "Perhaps the theft can come to some good in the village of Arnstadt. The villagers will have their lives back, but their homes and shops were ruined after two months of abandonment. Somebody ought to do something."

Keela looks at you with admiration. Together, the two of you ride off to her village, where you can eat and relax for a while and enjoy the peaceful life. In a few days, you will return to Arnstadt with kindness and caring as your gifts—and a priceless emerald collar, which will again bring hope to a village where once hope had been banished under the shadow of darkness.

Congratulations, hero.

The End